FIRE AND RAIN

JULIE MULHERN

J & M PRESS

Mulhern continues to depict the trappings of a privileged community...that blends a strong mystery with the demands of living in an exclusive society. Watching Ellison develop the strength of character to break through both her own and her society's expectations is a sheer delight."

– Kings River Life Magazine

"Mulhern's lively, witty sequel to *The Deep End* finds Kansas City, Mo., socialite Ellison Russell reluctantly attending a high school football game...Cozy fans will eagerly await Ellison's further adventures."

– Publishers Weekly

"What a fun read! Murder in the days before cell phones, the internet, DNA and AFIS."

– Books for Avid Readers

ACKNOWLEDGMENTS

Thanks to Matt. Forever and for always. And to Sally Berneathy, who is my village.

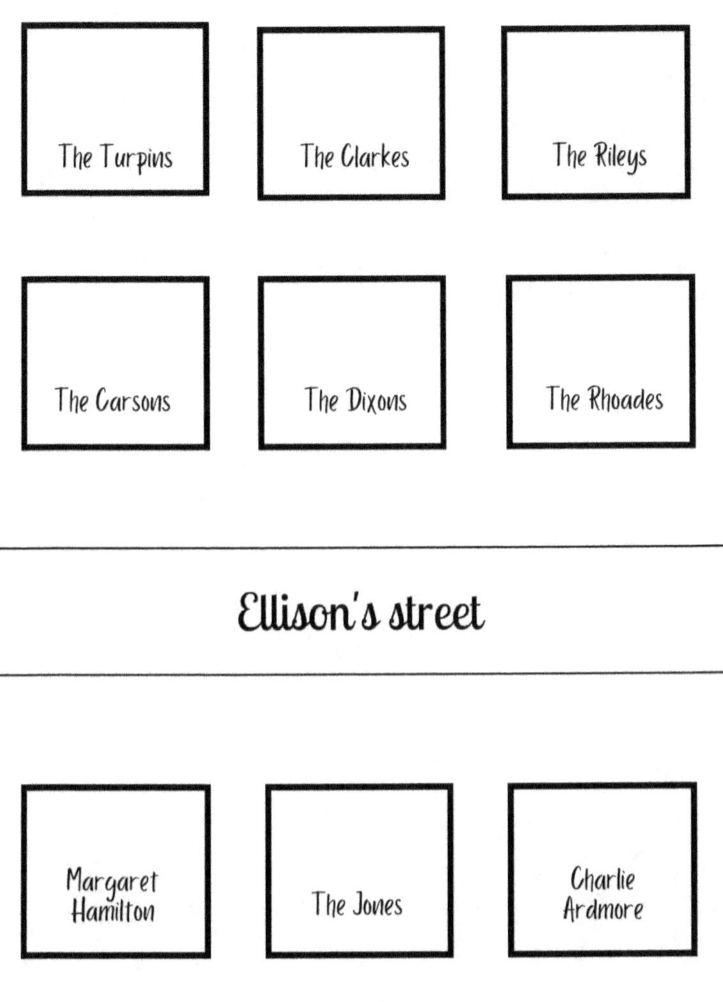
The Turpins
The Clarkes
The Rileys
The Carsons
The Dixons
The Rhoades
Ellison's street
Margaret Hamilton
The Jones
Charlie Ardmore

CHAPTER ONE

June, 1975
Kansas City, Missouri

"I spoke to Margaret about her boxwoods. I told her they need trimming. Do you know what she said to me?"

I leaned against the door frame and resisted pinching the space between my eyes. Barely. From the time I was old enough to toddle, Mother drilled respect for my elders, which meant that asking my across-the-street neighbor, Marian Dixon, to get the heck off my stoop wasn't an option.

But I wanted to. Badly.

"Do you know?" She raised her voice as if my silence vexed her.

I was the one who should be vexed. She'd parked herself on my doorstep without an invitation.

"Do you?"

She'd picked a fight with Margaret Hamilton? Marian was either incredibly brave or incredibly stupid. I guessed the latter.

I was half-convinced that my next-door neighbor was a witch. A double-double-toil-and-trouble, ride-a-broomstick witch. If Margaret cultivated hemlock and wolfsbane in her front yard, I'd maintain a polite smile and offer a cheery wave. I would not complain. "What did she say?"

"She told me I should mind my own business!"

Marian was lucky that Margaret hadn't hexed her. Wait! I narrowed my eyes. Was that a mustache growing above her upper lip? Had she always had those dark hairs?

"It is my business if the lawns on this block aren't maintained," she said.

The two cups of coffee I'd downed weren't near enough to deal with Marian so early in the morning. My mind wandered back to the kitchen where Mr. Coffee waited for me with a full pot. I imagined fresh coffee in a cup, a splash of cream, the slight bitterness exploding across my tastebuds—

"Ellison!"

Reluctantly, I let the vision of Mr. Coffee fade and focused on the woman in the navy blue skirt and white blouse with a Peter Pan collar who'd taken up residence on my stoop.

"Margaret's boxwoods!"

Marian needed a hobby. A hobby other than spying on her neighbors.

Clutching a clipboard, she scanned my lawn.

The hostas were lush, the yard was freshly mown, and geraniums rioted in the stone urns that flanked my front door. She couldn't possibly find fault.

"Even you have a better lawn." Marian was the queen of backhanded compliments. "Although—" she stroked her mustache "—red geraniums are a bit garish. Don't you think?"

Obviously not. I chose them.

Her gaze slid to my other next-door neighbor's front lawn, and she shrugged. "At least you planted flowers."

Charlie was a recently divorced doctor with a new job. He was too busy to fuss with his lawn or garden. And if he did plant flowers, his dog would decimate them in short order. Despite her name—Pansy—his golden had marked annuals as her sworn enemy. She dug up plants faster than anyone could put them in the ground. So, no flowers for Charlie. His sole nod to lawn maintenance was paying Tommy Oakes, a boy who lived down the street, to mow once a week. Tommy also mowed my yard. And Margaret's.

Tommy didn't clip hedges.

"I spoke with Jane about this," Marian said.

"The lack of flowers?

Marian screwed her flushed face into a frustrated scowl. "Margaret's hedges. Jane lives across the street from Margaret. She has to look at those hedges whenever she walks out her front door."

"What did Jane say?" Jane had three children, all of whom swam and played tennis and golf. The youngest, a girl, also took ballet lessons. Jane didn't have time to contemplate her neighbor's hedges. She didn't have time to contemplate her own hedges.

"She doesn't understand the seriousness of the problem."

My eyes ached with the need to roll. I bit the inside of my cheeks and held my tongue.

"It starts with little things."

I should have brought a cup of coffee with me when I answered the door. Additional caffeine might make this conversation less painful. Maybe. "It?"

"Anarchy."

"My husband?"

"Don't be ridiculous, Ellison. The decline of law and order."

She got the end of civilization from Margaret's shaggy hedge?

"The abandoning of social mores, polite society, and standards. Anarchy."

My husband's first name.

"We have to address this threat head on."

Oh, dear Lord. "If Margaret's bushes bother you that much, offer to clip them for her."

"I did." Marian's cheeks colored. "She said if I touched her hedge, she'd shove my clippers where the sun doesn't shine."

I clutched my throat, barely containing a bark of laughter.

"That's when I decided we need a petition."

A petition? I closed my eyes. If I ignored her long enough, maybe she'd go away.

"A petition demanding she trim her boxwoods." She jammed something sharp into my stomach.

"Oomph." I opened my eyes and looked down. Marian jammed me with her clipboard. Hard enough to leave a bruise. I rubbed a hand across my middle.

"Do you need a pen?"

"No."

"You have one?"

"I'm not signing a petition."

"Your mother would sign."

"Then start a signature drive on her block."

Marian's features pinched at my snark. "There's no need to be rude."

"I'm sure Margaret will trim the bushes on her own."

"I pointed out the problem last week, and she hasn't yet."

"Then complain to the homeowners' association." Margaret would be furious. With Marian. And the association. But not with me.

Marian hugged the clipboard to her chest. "The homeowners' association doesn't take this problem seriously."

The HOA didn't take Marian seriously. That's what happened when a person lodged a hundred complaints a week.

"Did Jane sign the petition?"

"No." Thunder settled on Marian's brow. "She asked me to return her sons' balls." Marian snorted as if the request were preposterous. "I warned those boys. 'Don't throw your balls into my yard.' Did they listen?"

"They're boys, Marian. They play catch. Sometimes a ball sails over a fence."

"They'll learn their lesson. Eventually. Olive's boys did." Olive and Quinn Rhoades were Marian's other next-door neighbors. Their sons, Oliver and Trey (Quinn Fairfax Rhoades III) were in college. Had they learned their lesson? More likely they'd outgrown tossing balls in the backyard.

Marian tsked. "They'll be moving soon."

I frowned. "The Rhoades?"

A sly smile curled her lips. "Marital trouble. I know the signs. There's a new car parked behind the house whenever Quinn travels for business."

Olive Rhoades delivered May baskets and homegrown tomatoes and Christmas fruitcakes to the widows who lived at either end of the block. She volunteered at a soup kitchen and the children's hospital and church. She had a kind word and a kinder smile for everyone she met. And if she looked for happiness away from her emotionally distant husband, it was nobody's business but her own.

I glanced at my watch and widened my eyes. "Is that the time?"

Marian's eyes narrowed. She didn't believe my ruse.

Not that I blamed her. As ruses went, exclaiming over the time was weak.

She thrust the clipboard at me.

I hid my hands behind my back. So adult. "I'm not signing that."

"But the hedge?" Her voice rose.

So many problems in the world. Real ones. And this woman spent her days spying on her neighbors and stirring up trouble.

"No. I'm sor—" I stopped myself. I would not apologize for my refusal. "I'm not signing. And now, I really must run, or I'll be late for a meeting."

She'd monitor my driveway to make sure I actually left.

Careful to keep Max, our Weimaraner, inside the house, I slipped through the storm door and offered a goodbye wave.

Marian's cheeks flushed. The rising heat or ire?

I shut the door on her. "She's a menace," I whispered to Max.

He sat on his haunches and stared at me with amber eyes.

"If she's not careful, someone will lose patience and murder her." It was a wonder someone hadn't already found a way to silence Marian. "Although, if the killer argued justifiable homicide at their trial, the jury would sympathize and sentence them to a slap on the wrist."

Max's tail wagged.

"You're bloodthirsty today."

He offered a doggy grin. With Marian gone, he could chase her cat unmolested.

"Don't be so happy. If someone kills Marian, I'll find her body." That was my life. Finding bodies. It wasn't fun.

Brnng, brnng.

What fresh hell was this? I ducked into my husband's office and picked up the receiver. "Hello."

"Ellison?" Mother's disapproval carried through the line. "Why isn't Aggie answering the phone?"

Had Mother called to talk to my housekeeper? Doubtful.

I girded my loins. "Aggie is at the market."

"Marian Dixon called me. She has a petition and wants your signature."

"Marian just left."

"Did you sign?"

"I did not."

"Why not?"

"What if she circulates a petition insisting I move?"

"Don't be ridiculous. She can't force you to sell your house."

"She can't force Margaret to trim her bushes. And between Marian and Margaret, I'd rather be on Marian's bad side." I perched on the edge of the desk and wrapped the phone's cord around my index finger. "Did you call about Marian and her petition, or is there something else?" I'd told Marian, who was sure to be watching my house, that I had a meeting. Now, I to leave my house for said imaginary meeting. If I didn't leave, and soon, she'd know I lied.

"Your father and I want you to join us for dinner tonight."

"It's Wednesday. Grace has a swim meet." Also known as hell masquerading as a kids' sporting event. And a very real reason to decline dinner.

"Then tomorrow night."

"Anarchy is working."

"You and Grace can come without him." She sounded pleased about that. Mother might accept my husband, but he wasn't her first choice for a son-in-law. She disapproved of his job.

"Grace has practice."

"She's done by five. We'll meet you at the club." Mother knew when Grace was done with practice, but she'd forgotten an actual meet? Doubtful. She'd managed me.

I couldn't win. Not without more coffee. I admitted defeat. "Fine."

"Five o'clock for cocktails. We'll eat at six."

~

Swim meets. I surveyed the pool deck and swallowed a sigh.

The good? Grace loved swimming, and I loved supporting

her. I'd been volunteering with the same women since Grace swam her first race. Those women had become friends, some of them close friends. Now that I was an old hand, volunteering gave me the opportunity to meet the young mothers, the women with a decade's worth of swim meets still in front of them. Also, I loved the way every soul on the pool deck would cheer for a struggling swimmer (usually seven, usually barely keeping afloat) to finish a race. I loved that child's smile when he or she pulled themselves out of the water and realized everyone had been cheering for them.

The bad? The concrete pool deck spent the day absorbing heat then held it like a jealous loner. Which meant the temperature was a few degrees hotter than hell. And heat like that made me prickly. Already my polo shirt (in the club's colors, of course) clung to my back.

The ugly? The heat made people drink. They downed gin and tonics like water, and the results weren't pretty. Also, there was something about watching their kids compete that brought out the worst in certain parents. Meets were supposed to be fun, not cause for tears.

Beau Riley was definitely trying not to cry. The eight-year-old boy was tan as a nut, and the summer sun had already bleached his blond hair almost white. He had big brown eyes (I had a weakness for brown eyes) and a ready smile. Beau Riley was not smiling now. Dampness blurred his brown eyes.

"You gave up at the end," said his father.

Whit Riley's grip on his son's arm looked painful. What was Whit doing here so early? Women worked the volunteer shifts, and their husbands showed up around five-thirty or six, made straight for the bar, then stood in the shade as their progeny competed.

"You're not some little girl," Whit whisper-yelled at his son.

Why was it when men wanted to convey their disdain for a weak male they compared him to a girl? *You throw like a girl. You run like a girl. You're a pus*—I couldn't bring myself to think it. Instead, I pasted on a tight smile. "He can't win every race, Whit."

For a half-second, rage filled Whit's eyes. How dare I interrupt him? "Sports are life lessons. Beau can't give up when things get difficult."

"They also teach us how to win and lose gracefully." A lesson Whit should remember. "They teach the need for hard work to achieve goals."

Whit's gaze cut to his son. "Someone hasn't been working hard enough."

Beau winced.

"And sometimes, no matter how hard we work, things don't go our way. Beau, I think your friends are waving for you to join them." I focused my gaze on Whit's grasp on his son's arm.

Slowly, finger by finger, Whit released his gasp.

"What's your next race?" I asked Beau.

He gulped and glanced at his father. "Backstroke."

"I'll be cheering for you."

"Thank you, Mrs. Russell." He offered me an apologetic smile. "I mean, Mrs. Jones."

"No worries," I assured him. "Have fun this afternoon."

Beau nodded and escaped his father.

"That was none of your business, Ellison." Whit Riley and his wife, Tippy, were high school sweethearts. As their classmate, I'd had a front-row seat to their teenage drama. Especially when I dated Whit's best friend, Grant Wycoff. I'd clutched Grant's hand while Whit's father belittled him for missing a basketball shot that would have won a game. I'd seen the pain in Whit's eyes. I'd pretended I didn't see his tears. I'd heard him swear he'd never, ever be like his dad. So why was he doing the same thing to his own son?

"You once told me you didn't want to be anything like your father."

"I'm nothing like him."

I lifted my brows. "Are you sure about that?"

The flush on Whit's cheeks wasn't due to the heat.

"Be better," I told him.

The announcer called the next race.

"Excuse me, Grace is swimming next. I want to cheer her on." I left Whit, ignoring the deep scowl that scored his forehead and tightened his mouth.

I found a spot at the edge of the pool and screamed like a lunatic for just under thirty seconds.

Grace hauled herself out of the water and flashed me a grin. She'd won.

I gave her a thumbs up, and she disappeared into a crowd of girls.

"Ellison?" Jane Carson stood beside me. "Do you have a minute?"

"For you? Of course."

We ceded the edge of the pool to parents with swimmers in the next race and found a tiny sliver of shade.

"What is Grace swimming today?"

"Breast, free, medley and free relay. What about your kids?"

"Will is swimming free, butterfly, and medley. He hates butterfly." Most kids did. "Jimmy swims breast, free, and back. Darcy swims free, back, medley, and free relay."

Jane had a busy afternoon.

She yanked on her ponytail. "I'm timing second shift."

"Me, too." I hated timing more than Will hated butterfly. The sun's relentless rays. The noise. The pressure of hitting the stopwatch at the right second. At least I'd have company in my misery.

She rubbed the back of her neck as if she already felt the coming misery. "Did Marian talk to you?"

Speaking of misery. "She did."

"Did you sign?"

"No." I checked our surroundings for random listeners. "I'd never cross Margaret that way."

"Marian has been erratic lately. It's scary. The boys were in the backyard yesterday evening and she yelled at them for being too loud. They're children and it wasn't yet seven o'clock. But she said she'd file a noise complaint."

"Maybe we'll get lucky, and Margaret will hex her."

"Turn her into a frog?"

"Or a stink bug."

Jane wiped a drip of sweat from her brow. "I wish I knew what set her off."

"Besides Margaret's hedge?"

"That darned hedge. If I never hear it mentioned again, it will be too soon." Jane rubbed the back of her neck. "Marian's always been difficult. But lately? She's impossible. This sounds awful, but I'm grateful she's focused on Margaret's hedge and not my boys. I'm sure that makes me a terrible person, but the woman's exhausting. Last weekend, while you were gone, she was positive there was someone lurking around her house. She had the police come. Three times. She even suggested that Will was responsible. They knocked on our door to check. Fortunately, Will was sleeping over at a friend's."

"What did Bill say?"

"He was livid. He told the police Marian is a menace." She glanced at the pool, and her expression morphed into shock. "Are we on free? Already? Can we talk later?" Without waiting for my reply, she hurried to the side of the pool and cheered loudly, as if volume might make up for missing most of the race.

I waved down a waiter and ordered an Arnold Palmer (I wanted a gin and tonic, but liquor and timing didn't mix).

"Hey, there." Lips brushed my bare neck.

I turned, and my heart skipped a beat. My husband was so damned handsome. His features were lean, his lips were delectable, and his eyes were the exact shade of coffee. "I didn't expect you."

"Grace asked me to come. Did I miss her race?"

"She won her race in breast stroke. Free is coming up." Swim meets were organized by stroke—breast, free, back, butterfly, medley, and free relay—then age group. A mother with a child in breast and free relay had to stay for hours to watch two races. One at the beginning, the other at the end. "After that, she's got medley and the relay."

He tugged at the collar of his white dress shirt. "It's hot out here."

"It's hell out here." I grabbed his hand and led him to a spot at the pool's side. "That's Corbin Clune in the pool. Grace's race is next."

We cheered as the girls dove off the blocks and cut through the water. Grace, who swam in lane four, took an early lead, but a swimmer from the other club closed the gap after the turn. "Go, Grace! Faster!"

"Good job, Grace! You've got this!" It was too early for most fathers to be here. Anarchy's was one of only a few men's voices.

Grace put on a burst of speed and touched the wall half a second before the other swimmer.

She slipped out of the water, slender and strong and smiling. Then she flashed us a grin.

Anarchy grinned back. "Well done!"

She headed toward us. "You came."

"I wouldn't miss it."

My chest felt too small to hold my heart. This, right here, was why I tolerated swim meets. Because they brought people together.

"I have two more races."

"I'll be here," Anarchy replied. "Cheering."

"Mom will be timing."

"Don't remind me."

Grace's smile broadened. "At least when you're timing, you don't miss my races."

"That happened once." More than once. More than ten times.

"Whatever, Mom. I'm glad you're both here."

Anarchy claimed my sweaty palm in his cool fingers, and I looked up at him with hearts shining in my eyes. "Me, too."

CHAPTER TWO

The successful conclusion of a swim meet meant a party. A family party. With little ones dashing here, there, and everywhere. Thirteen-year-old girls eyeing largely clueless fourteen-year-old boys. And older teenagers pretending sophistication they didn't yet possess.

The dinner buffet featured tacos with mildly spiced ground beef, lettuce, diced tomatoes, and shredded cheese. Two kinds of salsa (green for the brave). Rice, refried beans, and an array of cookies and ice cream bars filled out the menu. Mothers who'd downed gin and tonics all afternoon switched to margaritas (because tequila brought out the best in all of us).

Children filled their plates and ate cross-legged on their damp beach towels. Their parents, exhausted by heat and mixed drinks, gathered around wrought-iron tables. A few hopeful women tried ordering salads only to be told the buffet was open, but the kitchen was closed.

The swim coaches, kids who'd participated in country club swim before they graduated from high school, had a table of their own. As college students, they had a glamor that mesmerized young swimmers. They looked effortlessly cool, both literally and figuratively.

Heat and humidity draped my shoulders like a mink stole. Not the best feeling in the summer, but bearable with the sun's disappearance.

Anarchy and I shared a table with Jane and Bill, both of whom poked at their dinners.

I patted my face with a paper napkin and took another sip of ice water.

"Are these things always so hot?" asked Anarchy.

Jane barked a laugh. "Just wait till championships in July." She turned to me. "At least Grace is swimming A. The B championship is the longest day of my year." Every swimmer got a chance to compete. That meant at least six heats of seven-year-old girls crawling the crawl. Then another six heats of seven-year-old boys.

Jimmy appeared at his mother's side. "Is it time to go home yet?"

"Don't you want to stay for the awards?"

Jimmy shook his head. He'd wrapped a damp towel around his narrow waist, and, impossibly in the heat, his teeth chattered.

"What about the party?" The way Jane said "party," made a disco ball and lights sound like a not-to-be-missed event. "They have a DJ."

The coaches would present awards then dance with the youngest kids.

"I'll take you home," said Bill. On its surface, it seemed a kind offer. But it left Jane with two kids who'd be overtired and fractious by the time she insisted they leave.

"You don't want to collect your ribbons?" Jane asked.

"I guess I might stay for that," Jimmy allowed. Grudgingly. As if his mother was impeding his fun.

As darkness fell, the coaches gathered the swimmers into a

circle. They recognized kids who'd beat their best times. "Now," said the head coach. "For the swimmer of the week. This is a swimmer who always tries his best. He encourages everyone in the pool at practice, cheers for his team, and makes it fun for us to be here."

The coach paused, letting the tension build, and the kids leaned in, as if they hadn't heard the same praise heaped on last week's swimmer of the week.

"The swimmer of the week is Beau Riley."

The parents applauded. Politely. Except for me. I hooted my approval.

Beau, who wore an enormous grin, stumbled up to the coaches and accepted his tee-shirt.

I searched for Whit in the darkness. Would he ease up on his son now that he'd been recognized?

Jimmy, who now clutched a handful of yellow ribbons, asked, "Can we go, now?"

Bill pushed away from the table. "That's my cue." He took his son's hand and led him toward the parking lot.

Jane sighed. "I should find Will and Darcy and put them on notice. We're not staying late. Please, excuse me." She left us.

"This is nice." Anarchy stretched out his legs and surveyed the pool deck.

"This?"

"You. Me. A starry night."

"I smell bad."

"You look pretty."

"Half the people here are zonkered." I swirled the last of my margarita. I was not zonkered. One drink. One. That's all I allowed myself before I drove.

With a yell probably heard in Nebraska, a twelve-year-old boy cannon-balled into the pool. Water from his splash soaked my shoes.

"The kids are so excited," Anarchy observed.

"The young ones. Grace is probably already gone."

"Swim meets bring out the glass-half-empty side of your personality."

"Very funny."

The DJ played his first song and my head sank into my hands.

"What?" asked Anarchy.

"You haven't lived until you watch nine-year-olds do the hustle."

His lips quirked. "There's Grace." He waved, and she approached our table. She wore cut-off jean shorts (short enough to give her grandmother a heart attack) over her team suit and carried her pool bag. "Congratulations."

She grinned. "Thank you."

"What's your plan?" I asked.

We were distracted by a boy making up his own dance moves. Enterprising. But a bad idea in a line dance. The resulting collision downed three dancers.

"Slumber party at Debbie's."

"Her mother knows?"

"Yes."

"You're leaving now?" I nodded toward her waiting friends.

"Yep."

"Have fun."

She dropped a kiss on my cheek, hesitated, offered Anarchy the same, then disappeared with her girlfriends.

Anarchy pressed his hand to his cheek where Grace had kissed him. "She's a good kid."

"The best. Are you ready?" I stood. I wanted a cool shower, crisp sheets, and a good night's sleep.

Anarchy claimed my elbow. "I'll walk you to your car."

"Thank you." Country club parking lots were positively fraught with danger. Especially at night. I might be shot or stabbed or conked on the head. No exaggeration.

"Ellison?" Daisy, who had a child on her left hip while she used her right hand to hold another, nodded at Anarchy. "You're not leaving?"

"We are," I replied. Then I frowned. I played bridge with Daisy every week. The woman had no poker face. I could tell the cards in her hand by her expression. And right now, the crease in Daisy's forehead said she was worried. "What's wrong?"

She caught her lip in her teeth.

I waited.

"Mom." The child whose hand she held danced from foot to foot. "I have to potty."

"Okay, honey. Ellison, I'll call you."

"I can wait."

"No, no. Go on. It's not that important."

"You're sure?"

She nodded and headed toward the bathroom.

"Ready?" asked Anarchy.

So ready. "Yes."

Together, we walked to the parking lot, strolling through rows of station wagons which belonged to women, and luxury sedans and sports cars which belonged to their husbands.

Anarchy opened the driver's door to my TR6 and waited as I sank into the seat. Then he closed my door, leaned over, and kissed me. A lingering kiss that curled my toes. "See you at home."

I sped down the club's winding drive with the car's top still down. The warm night air tugged at strands of my hair and carried the scent of possibility.

My life had changed so much in a year. Last June, I'd been unhappily married. Now? Now, the wind stole a delighted laugh from my lips.

I'd married the "right" man shortly after I earned my art degree, and we had settled into a comfortable life.

Comfortable, not remotely happy.

The fizziness in my veins, the smile on my lips, and the rose-colored glasses perched on my nose—they were all thanks to Anarchy.

I turned up the radio and sang with Toni Tennille. Love would keep us together. Forever.

I pulled into the driveway, and my headlights caught movement. Golden movement.

"Pansy?" I got out of the car and took a small step toward the escaped dog.

She wagged her tail and grinned at me.

I pushed the loose strands of hair away from my face and groaned. Pansy, unsupervised, might dig up half the neighborhood.

"Come."

Her grin widened.

"Treat."

Her tail wagged, but she didn't move.

I took a slow step toward her and upped my game. "Bacon."

She danced backward on muddy paws as if she'd been waiting for someone to join in her second-favorite game. Chase. Destruction was her favorite game. And if her paws were any indication, she'd played a few rounds by herself.

"Pansy!"

She grinned at me then raced across the street to Marian's house.

"Pansy!"

She ignored me.

"Charlie!"

Charlie didn't answer.

In the time it took me to fetch her owner, Pansy might shred Marian's impatiens or destroy her non-garish salmon geraniums. If Pansy damaged Marian's hollyhocks, the woman would have a faunching fit. Not a petition kind of fit. An animal control kind of fit.

I sped across the street, ran up the Dixons' drive, and raced around their house to the backyard.

"Pansy! Oh!" I pressed my palm to my chest. "Leonard."

Marian's husband gaped at me. He stood next to a Lincoln with an open trunk. Three large suitcases gathered at his feet. "Ellison, what are you doing?"

"Sorry about this." I wasn't given to trespassing. "Charlie's dog." I pointed an accusing finger at Pansy. "She'll dig up Marian's flowers."

Leonard and I shared a wince.

"Can you catch her?" he asked.

"I can try." I lunged forward, but Pansy danced away from me.

If Leonard was startled by my sudden appearance, the curse hovering on the tip of my tongue might give him palpitations. I sealed my lips.

"What are you going to do?" he asked.

"Pansy." I held out my hand. "Be a good girl."

She laughed at me.

"Hold on." Leonard disappeared through the back door, returning a moment later with a beef jerky stick. "Here." He put the stick in my hand.

Pansy drooled.

"Beef jerky." I waved the dried meat slowly, and her head followed the trajectory.

Catching her was suddenly easy. With my fingers wrapped around her collar, I asked, "Are you leaving town?"

"Yes."

"Vacation?"

"Yes."

"How marvelous." The block could use several days without

Marian. Would it be obvious if I asked how long they'd be gone? "Where are you going?"

"New York."

"I've heard wonderful things about *Chicago*. It just opened. Do you know John Kander? He wrote the music." And he grew up in Kansas City.

Leonard hefted the first suitcase into the trunk. "I'm a busy man, I don't have time for Broadway." Or me. He didn't say that, but I heard it in his tone.

I retreated a step, still holding Pansy's collar for dear life. "Well, thanks for the jerky. Have a nice trip." I dragged Pansy down the Dixons' drive, crossed the street, and jammed a finger at Charlie's doorbell. Then I waited.

Anarchy pulled into our drive and called, "What are you doing?"

"Pansy was roaming."

"Uh-oh." That was an understatement. "Do you need help?"

"If Charlie's not home, we'll have to keep her." It was a sobering thought. I jabbed the bell a second time, and Charlie yanked open the door. His hair was mussed. His shirt was buttoned incorrectly. And he had the look of a man who'd been interrupted. One who was ready to yell.

I didn't care if he yelled. I was too grateful to care about volume. "Pansy got out. I caught her in the Dixons' backyard."

He paled.

"Before she did any damage."

"Thank you." He glanced at Marian's house and rubbed his palms up and down his face. "So much."

"Her paws are dirty, so you may be hearing from someone." That was a certainty.

"At least it won't be Marian." He frowned at Pansy. "How did you get out?"

She looked at him with adoring eyes and wagged her tail.

He glanced over his shoulder and yelled, "Libba!"

My best friend, who wore Charlie's lab coat and nothing else, descended the front stairs. Had they been playing doctor? Never mind. I didn't want to know.

"Did you let Pansy out?" Charlie demanded.

Libba offered up a flirty smile. "I put her in the backyard. I don't like her watching us." Her gaze shifted to me. "She stands by the side of the bed and wags her tail. It's distracting."

Charlie blushed. Deeply.

It was me who asked, "Did you check the gate?"

She winced, and there was a long pause before she admitted, "No. I'm sorry."

Charlie took a leash from the coat tree near his front door, stepped outside, and clipped the leash onto Pansy's collar. "Thanks for this, Ellison."

"You're welcome." I turned to go home.

"Did Marian stop by your house earlier?" he asked.

I paused. "She did."

"Did you sign her petition?"

"I did not. You?"

"Hell, no." He rubbed his chin. "Margaret Hamilton is terrifying." He had that right. "I can't help but think that one of these days Marian is going to tick off the wrong person."

I shivered.

"Are you cold?"

"No. A goose walked over my grave." There was a shower waiting for me. And my husband. But I paused long enough to share the good news with Charlie. "When I was across the street, I talked to Leonard. He was packing the car for a vacation in New York."

"Hallelujah."

"Are you sure he's taking Marian?" asked Libba.

"There were three suitcases."

"Maybe he's leaving her," she suggested.

Marian, without Leonard to temper her excesses, would be unbearable. I groaned.

Libba grinned at me. "Maybe someone will bump her off and you can find the body."

That was a bit too close to my own thoughts. "Remind me why we're friends."

"I know all your secrets," Libba replied.

"Likewise."

"You just think you do." She wrinkled her nose. "It's a shame."

"That I don't know everything?"

"No, silly. That Marian's death won't make the *New York Times*."

"What are you talking about?"

"A dead pool."

I stared at her.

"Don't act so surprised. People drop like flies around you."

"I don't know what a dead pool is."

"It's a betting game. I think it started in Indianapolis."

Charlie wrapped an arm around Libba's waist and pulled her close. "Honey, what are you talking about?"

"It started at the Speedway," she explained. "The race was dangerous. People bet on who'd win and who'd die."

I pinched the bridge of my nose. "That's positively ghoulish."

She shrugged. "My point is, I'd bet on Marian dying, but she doesn't warrant coverage in the *Times*. We get five picks. I usually select an old actor, a young musician, a politician, and two others."

I gaped at her.

"Who did you pick?" asked Charlie.

"Elvis, Alice Cooper, Ari Onassis, Jimmy Hoffa, and Agatha Christie."

"How do you decide?"

"I read. If they're taking drugs, fascinated by death, crossing the mafia, or old, they're good options."

"They're people."

"Yes."

"And you bet they'll die."

"I didn't make the game, I just play it. Besides, we all die. My point is—if Marian were famous, I'd bet on her death."

oof!

I slit an eye and saw only darkness. What did Max want in the middle of the night? Determined to ignore him, I snuggled deeper into my pillow.

Woof! My dog was nothing if not determined.

"Shush," I told him.

Woof! He ignored me. No surprise there.

I slit the other eye and found the clock's red glow. "It's three in the morning. Go back to bed."

Woof! The bark demanded my attention. My immediate attention.

"Stop it." Why not let me sleep? The swim meet and its after-party had left me exhausted. I pulled a pillow over my head and felt the mattress next to me shift. "Don't do it," I warned my husband. "If he knows you'll get up whenever he asks, he'll never stop asking." Max was a give-him-an-inch-he'll-take-ten-miles kind of dog.

Next to me, Anarchy stilled, but I felt his tension. "He doesn't usually bark like this."

Woof!

"I think he senses something." Anarchy didn't sound sleepy. He sounded alert. How did he do that in the middle of the night?

"Probably a rabbit or a squirrel."

"I'll check." Anarchy threw off the light blanket, strode to the window, and gasped.

"What is it?" My skin prickled. "What's wrong?"

"The Dixons' house is on fire." He'd already left the window and replaced his pajama bottoms with pants.

Woof. Max's bark had a smug I-told-you-so quality.

I ignored Max's gloating and told Anarchy, "They just left for a vacation."

Anarchy flipped on a light and slipped his feet into a pair of loafers. "So, the house is empty?"

"Yes. Well, maybe. I might be wrong. Leonard was packing the car when I saw him." I caught my lip in my teeth. "I'm pretty sure he pulled out of the drive as I was dragging Pansy to Charlie's house." I pushed my hair out of my face and joined him at the window.

"Was Marian in the car?"

The Dixons' roof was engulfed in flame and the fire lit the night.

I'd caught only a glimpse of the car. My attention had been on Pansy. "I don't know."

"Call the fire department," Anarchy instructed.

I hurried to the phone and dialed. Arson? I hated that my first thought was so cynical, but when a person found bodies as often as I did, the rose-colored glasses slipped.

"What's your emergency?" The woman who answered my call sounded cool as a cucumber, even slightly bored.

"My neighbor's house is on fire."

"Address please."

I gave it to her.

"Is anyone in the home?"

"I don't know. They were planning a vacation, but I'm not sure if they've left yet." I glanced around the bedroom and realized Anarchy had disappeared.

If he planned on watching Marian's house burn, I'd be at his side.

"I have to go." I hung up the phone, pulled on a pink seersucker robe, and jammed my feet into a worn pair of Tretorns.

Maybe standing outside while my neighbor's house was reduced to ash made me ghoulish. I preferred to think I was concerned. Also, the entire neighborhood had gathered at the end of my drive so many times I'd lost count. And Marian had been at the front of the crowd each time. For once, my house wasn't the center of attention, and I intended to be a member of the audience rather than the star player.

I descended the front stairs and found the front door unlocked. "You stay here," I told Max. He'd followed me down the stairs, ready to investigate.

He gazed at me with wounded amber eyes. How could I deny him this adventure?

"I know you spotted the fire." I smoothed my hands down his silken ears. "You're a regular hero. But it may be chaotic outside." Chasing Max, which was a certainty, across multiple front yards would only add to the chaos.

Woof! He disagreed.

"No." I ignored my dog's scowl and slipped through the front door just in time to see my husband take off his tee-shirt, wrap it around his hand, and punch out a window to the Dixons' sun porch. He reached inside, unlocked the sash, opened the window, and disappeared into a burning building.

My heart stopped.

Stopped.

No beats.

Nor could I breathe. No air into my lungs. No air out.

Black spots danced at the edge of my vision.

Despite the fire raging across the street and the night's warmth, ice ran through my veins and a bone-deep shiver traveled through my body. I couldn't lose him. And I couldn't go after him. I'd be a liability in a fire, not an asset.

The pain in my heart stabbed deeper, and I slid my violently shaking fingers into the robe's pockets. How could he do this to me? To Grace?

Sirens pierced the night, and I welcomed their shrill sound.

The door behind me opened, and Grace emerged. The fire reflected in her eyes as she scanned our yard. "Where's Anarchy?"

Despite the heavy humidity, the air seemed too thin. I still couldn't breathe, couldn't speak. I pointed at the inferno.

Her mouth rounded in horror, and she pressed her palms against her chest, as if her hands had the power to contain the sudden fear in her heart. "You let him run into a burning building?"

Let him? If he'd asked me, I'd have told him to sit his heroic hiney down on our front stoop to wait for the firemen. He hadn't given me the chance. I fought back a hysterical giggle, and air snuck past my closed throat and into my lungs. "He didn't ask for my permission."

A firetruck squealed to a stop at the curb.

"Mom." Grace's hand circled my wrist, and she tugged on me. "You need to tell them he's inside."

She was right. Absolutely right.

We raced down the front walk as fire ate through what was left of the Dixons' roof and lit each window with an evil glow. Anarchy was in that house. The roof might collapse. He might be trapped. He might burn. Blood rushed to my ears, and I stumbled. There was no way anyone could survive that fire. I pressed one hand to my chest and the other to my mouth and made my feet move faster.

Before I reached the fire engine, the Dixons' front door flew open and a man who clutched something in his arms stumbled onto their lawn.

Acrid smoke poured from the house, making it hard to see clearly, but that was my husband. It had to be. I raced across the street. To him. With Grace at my heels.

Anarchy collapsed onto his knees, coughed hard enough to wrench his shoulders, and dropped his bundle. Marian's cat streaked into the darkness.

I knelt next to him as my brain struggled with what I'd just seen. I blinked through smoky tears and clutched Anarchy's hand. "Are you hurt?"

He shook his head and coughed.

Not hurt. Fully alive. A spark lit in my soul. "You saved the cat?"

He had the scratches on his hands and arms to prove it. Apparently, the frightened animal had wanted to remain in the burning house.

"You risked your life for Marian's horrible cat?" The spark caught fire and burned me from within. How. Could. He?

"I broke in to see if the Dixons needed help. You didn't sound sure about their vacation. The stairs were impassable." He coughed again, and his eyes streamed.

Saving people made the risk marginally better. But it didn't matter why he'd run into the blazing house. I wouldn't survive losing him. Didn't he understand that?

I clasped my hands and forced my breathing to slow. Yelling like a fishwife would accomplish nothing. Anarchy was the type of man who ran into burning buildings. I had solid proof of that now.

Another deep breath. I only needed a few thousand to calm down completely.

"Ellison?"

I gazed at his handsome, soot-stained face. He was a hero. My hero. How could I ask him to be less?

Grace, who wore a fearsome scowl she must have learned from her grandmother, poked him in the ribs. "You had us worried. Mom needs you. I need you. Don't do that again."

She'd demanded what I couldn't. And I wasn't remotely upset about it.

Anarchy still rested on his knees, with his back bent into a "C," but he nodded. "No more running into burning buildings. I promise."

I tightened my grip on his hand. "I'll hold you to that."

Firemen swarmed and one approached us. "Are you hurt?"

Anarchy answered with a quick shake of his head. "No."

"Is this your house?"

I pointed to our house. "We live there."

"I'm a cop," Anarchy rasped. "I tried…I tried to get to the second floor, but the stairs are on fire."

"Are there people inside?" asked the fireman.

"We don't know," I replied. "They may be on vacation."

At the curb, another fireman attached a hose to the hydrant. Not that water would do much good now. Fire raged through the entire structure.

"Let's get you to safety," said the fireman.

I glanced at the street where the neighbors gathered. Their curious faces said the burning house was the star of this drama, but Anarchy, Grace, and I were supporting players. I'd bet good money that somewhere someone was on the phone with Mother (usually Marian's job, but I was sure someone had stepped in for her). If they weren't telling Mother about our disheveled presence on the Dixons' lawn, they were reporting Grace's tiny nightie.

I helped Anarchy to his feet, and Grace grabbed his other elbow.

He didn't need us, but neither of us was willing to let him go. With the grace of drunken entrants in a three-legged race, we lurched to the curb.

"Ellison." Whit, who'd taken the time to don actual clothes, eyed me with suspicion, as if I'd suddenly developed a taste for arson. "What happened?"

"The Dixons' house is on fire," I deadpanned.

Grace tittered.

Whit scowled at us both. "I can see that. How?"

How would I know? Before I crafted a suitably sarcastic reply, a fireman with his arms spread wide stepped toward us. "Folks, if you'll head to the other side of the street, please? We want you out of harm's way."

As a group, my family and my neighbors retreated to my front yard where we watched fireman direct water through Marian's windows as they trampled her flowers.

Flames reached high into the night sky and showers of embers dusted the Rhoades' and Carsons' houses. Olive whimpered and clutched her hands, and her husband strode toward the firemen and gestured wildly.

The firemen redirected their hoses to the Dixons' neighbors' roofs.

Tippy wrung her hands. "This is just awful. This is supposed to be a quiet neighborhood. Instead, there are murders. And now a fire."

Margaret Hamilton, who'd snuck up on us, sneered at her. "Are you concerned about property values or the Dixons' welfare?"

Tippy straightened her shoulders. "Don't give me that look, Margaret. Of course I care about Marian and Leonard. But you know just as well as I do that normal people don't find bodies every other week."

I winced. Arguably, there had been way too many murders and attempted murders on our block. But it wasn't my fault. Try telling that to my neighbors. They seemed to think I was a magnet for death.

Margaret looked down her long nose. "Are you suggesting the fire is Ellison's fault?"

Tippy rolled her eyes, as if the ever-present threat of Margaret's hexes didn't concern her. "Of course not. Right now, I don't care how the fire started. If the wind shifts, my home might burn."

She wasn't wrong. Even with water pouring on their roofs, with the wind blowing from the west, her house and the Rhoades' home were in danger.

The firemen were impressive, working as a unit until they had the flames under control.

I rested my head on Anarchy's shoulder. "What happens next?"

"An investigator will come and determine if the fire was accidental or arson."

"Arson?"

He nodded, the expression on his handsome face grim.

"They'll want to talk to you, find out what you saw."

"Yes."

"What did you see?"

He leaned closer to me and whispered, "I think I saw a body."

Mother sailed across the veranda at the club, offering regal nods to those already seated. With the briefest of nods, she approved the table overlooking the pool, then sank onto her chair like a queen taking her throne.

"You're sure you won't be too warm?" my father asked her.

"It's a perfect evening," she replied.

Well, perfect if you enjoyed the feeling of perspiration tricking between your breasts. I, for one, did not. But I wasn't about to argue with her choice of tables. She was in a mood.

Hector, the assistant manager who'd led us to the table, asked, "What may I get you to drink?"

"Tom Collins," Mother told him.

"Two," said Daddy.

"Make that three, please." I glanced at the empty chair. "Grace will want a Tab with lime."

"Of course, Mrs. Russell." With a deferential nod (for Mother's benefit, not mine), he left us and headed for the bar.

"How much longer will Grace swim?" Daddy's gaze tracked Grace's progress through the water as he took off his tie, a pink madras plaid that Mother had selected for him, and slipped it into the pocket of his blue blazer.

"Did she bring appropriate clothes for dinner?" Mother asked.

"She did." A Lilly Pulitzer shift that was sure to meet Mother's exacting standards hung in Grace's locker.

Mother shifted her gaze to me, and the tightness around her lips said I'd somehow failed to meet her standards.

My make-up was perfect. Barely there nudes. None of the blue eyeshadow or frosted lipstick that Mother found so tacky. In truth, I wasn't a fan of that blue eyeshadow either and had sent Grace upstairs to wash her face more than once.

I patted my hair, which was held in a neat French twist.

Not the make-up. Not the hair. That left the dress. She did not like my dress. If her expression was anything to go by, she actively disapproved. A deep sigh escaped her tight lips. "You look so lovely in softer colors."

I'd bought the black halter dress on my honeymoon in Italy. I'd paired it with gold chains and sandals. A black cotton cardigan hung on the back of my chair. If Mother had chosen to eat inside in the air conditioning, the cardigan would have covered my bare shoulders (which were presumably the problem). "I picked this up in Italy."

"So very European." She did not mean European in the

elegant, royal, Princess Grace of Monaco way. No, she meant European in the slutty, Catherine Deneuve in *Belle de Jour* way.

"I like it," I replied.

The tension at the table was suddenly thicker than the humidity. And that was saying something.

Daddy glanced between his wife and daughter then stretched his legs and crossed his tan ankles. "Tell us about the fire, Ellison."

Really? That was the topic he'd chosen to redirect Mother? "The Dixons' house is gone," I told them. All that remained were the brick chimneys and a portion of the back wall. "When I left earlier today, the fire marshal was waiting for the ashes to cool."

Mother's brows lifted. "To cool?"

"Before they searched for bodies." Not for one minute did I think Anarchy was wrong about a body.

She shuddered.

"There's an excellent chance the Dixons are on vacation," I added.

Mother pursed her lips and scanned the veranda for the waiter with our drinks. "Disaster follows you, Ellison."

"What are you suggesting?"

"The fire was across the street from your house."

Mother knew I hadn't started that fire, and I ought to be grateful she wasn't scolding me about Grace's nightie, but I couldn't stop myself from asking, "You think the Dixons' house burned because it was close to mine?"

The purse on Mother's lips deepened until she looked like a duck.

"Frannie." Daddy patted her hand. "Ellison had nothing to do with that fire."

Mother huffed softly, then her eyes widened.

I turned in my chair and followed her gaze.

Anarchy strode toward our table.

"Ellison." Mother's voice held enough censure to fill the club swimming pool. "Get hold of yourself."

The sun glinted off Anarchy's hair and kissed his shoulders. Behind his sunglasses, I was sure his eyes were twinkling. "What do you mean?"

"You're grinning like a loon. Act your age, not your shoe size."

My shoe size. That would be a seven. What I had in mind wasn't for seven-year-olds.

"She's in love, Frannie," said Daddy.

"She doesn't need to broadcast that to the entire club."

"He's my husband. We're newly married. We're in love."

Mother arched a brow. Being married and being in love weren't necessarily linked. "After that rushed courtship, I'm sure there are people who assume your family is growing." Her gaze dropped to my lap.

"I will not be providing more grandchildren."

"That's good, because I'm done babysitting."

When had she ever, ever babysat? I bit my tongue to keep from asking.

"Frances." Anarchy smiled at Mother. "Nice to see you. Harrington." He extended his hand, and Daddy shook it.

"Anarchy, what a pleasure." Mother didn't sound at all pleased. "Ellison told us you were unable to join us this evening, that you were working."

"I am. May I?"

Mother stared at Grace's empty chair as if she wished with her whole being that Anarchy hadn't suggested joining us. With a resigned wave, she motioned for him to sit. "What work brings you to the club?"

"Questions. For Ellison."

"For me?" I tilted my head and stared at him.

"Can you remember your conversation with Dixon?"

"For the most part."

"He said he was traveling to New York? By car?"

"I assumed he was going to the airport." Driving to New York sounded awful. Driving in New York sounded worse.

"Was Marian going with him?"

"He didn't say." The Dixons had never taken separate vacations before. No golf trips for him. No spa trips for her.

The waiter arrived with our cocktails. "Something to drink, sir?"

"Iced tea, please."

My first sip of my Tom Collins was tart and refreshing. Too bad it curdled in my stomach. Anarchy wouldn't be here asking questions about the Dixons unless he was right. Someone died in the fire. "They found a body."

He nodded.

Mother's face pinched as if she'd bitten into a lemon, and Daddy pinched the bridge of his nose. Their strained expressions made it obvious that they were containing soul-deep Ellison-did-it-again sighs.

"Marian or Leonard?" I asked.

"The coroner says it's a man's body. We haven't identified him yet." He glanced at my parents. "Please keep that to yourselves."

Daddy nodded, then prompted, "Frannie."

"Of course. I never gossip."

I wasn't touching that comment with a ten-foot pole. Instead, I asked, "Was it murder?"

"The arson investigator from the fire department says the fire was set."

Mother glared at me as if I'd snuck over to the Dixons' home and lit the match. "Really, Ellison? Another murder?"

CHAPTER FOUR

From his spot on the counter, Mr. Coffee offered me a saucy wink. *Another cup?*

"Need you ask?" Mother's disposition hadn't improved when Anarchy left us last night. And proximity to her mood had led me to order an extra cocktail. This morning, I was feeling the aftereffects.

I rose from my seat at the kitchen island and wrapped my fingers around Mr. Coffee's pot. The sweet sound of his nectar splashing into my mug was more heavenly than a host of angels singing.

How was dinner last night?

I sipped. "Much as you'd expect. Mother was in rare form, and Anarchy stopped by."

The club? If Mr. Coffee had eyebrows, they'd reach the top of his gingham face.

"He had questions about the fire. There was a body."

Marian or Leonard?

"Not Marian. It's a man."

So, Leonard?

"It seems that way."

Brngg, brngg.

I held up a finger to forestall Mr. Coffee's next question, then answered the phone. "Hello."

"Ellison? It's Jinx."

I suppressed a tired sigh. "Good morning."

"Is it true?" Jinx ignored the pleasantries.

"Is what true?" I played stupid.

"Is Leonard Dixon dead?"

"You heard about the body?" It was a silly question. Jinx knew all the gossip. Always. She even knew about the body. What she didn't know was who'd died. That was why she was calling me.

The back door opened, and Aggie and Max stepped inside. My housekeeper wore a bright orange and lime green kaftan in a geometric pattern. Enormous hoops hung from her ear lobes, and her curly red hair hung in wild corkscrews around her face. Aggie's cheeks were flushed an attractive pink, and her eyes sparkled as if she had a juicy secret. "I'm so glad you're up. I just talked to—" her eyes widened when she noticed the receiver in my hand "—sorry."

"Jinx, may I call you back?"

"Just tell me. Is it Marian?"

"I honestly don't know." Just a small fib. I knew it wasn't Marian, but Anarchy wouldn't want me divulging details of his investigation.

"Anarchy hasn't told you?"

"Not a peep."

She groaned her displeasure. "Call me back. Don't forget."

"Promise." I returned the receiver to its cradle, then turned to Aggie. "You were saying?"

"I just talked to Florence."

Max sat at my feet and regarded me with enormous, I'm-a-good-dog eyes.

When I didn't move, he gave me an I-spotted-the-fire whine.

"Fine." I stood and reached for the treat jar on top of the refrigerator, the only place we'd found where he couldn't help himself to biscuits when our backs were turned. "Who is Florence?"

"She's the Rhoades' housekeeper."

"I see." That our housekeepers gossiped was a disconcerting idea. I handed over Max's biscuit, and he took his prize to the dog mat in the corner and munched happily.

Aggie frowned as if she had read my thoughts. "I never discuss you or Grace or Anarchy." She pressed her right hand to her chest. "I swear."

I believed her. "Thank you."

"Florence says there was only one body in the house."

"Florence is well informed."

"Observant. They only carried out one body bag. She also says Mr. Dixon was having an affair. A serious one. He planned on leaving his wife, and she killed him."

"Wow. How does Florence know about the affair?" If she was right, her theory wasn't outlandish.

"She overheard them fighting."

"When?"

"A few weeks ago."

"How?"

"She was serving cocktails on the screened porch."

"So Olive and Quinn also heard?"

"Yes."

"What exactly did Florence hear?"

"Mrs. Dixon said she knew the truth, and if Mr. Dixon thought he could leave her, he had another think coming. She told him she'd never be a pathetic divorcee spritzing perfume at Woolf Brothers or selling clothes at Harzfeld's to women who used to be her friends." Aggie shook her head. "There's dignity in any honest work."

"Agreed." But the necessity of earning a paycheck was hard

on ladies who'd done little with their lives but lunch. Or, in Marian's case, spy on her neighbors.

Aggie pushed her unruly curls away from her face. "She said she'd see him dead before she let that happen to her."

"How did Leonard respond?"

Aggie gave an apologetic shrug. "Mr. Dixon wasn't as loud as Mrs. Dixon." Meaning Florence hadn't heard his reply. "Florence said Mr. and Mrs. Rhoades were agog."

I easily imagined Olive leaning in to better make out the Dixons' conversation.

"When they realized Florence had caught them listening, Mr. Rhoades called their dog. Loudly. After that, the Dixons were quiet."

"I bet. Anarchy will want to know about this."

"He left for work an hour ago."

Which explained why I'd awakened to find his side of the bed cold. "That's okay. We'll call him."

Anarchy and I walked to the Clarkes' house for Sally's dinner party.

"We could have cut through," I observed. The Clarkes, Sally and her husband Ward, lived behind the Dixons, and it wasn't as if Marian was around to object if we cut through her yard.

Instead, we'd avoided the trampled grass and the burnt and blackened remains of their home and strolled around the block.

Anarchy claimed my hand and gave my fingers a quick squeeze. "Remind me about our hosts."

"Sally and Ward were at our wedding reception."

He paused on the sidewalk and cocked a brow. "There were a million people at our reception."

A slight exaggeration. "Ward is a stockbroker. Sally volunteers."

"For?"

"The Junior League, the children's hospital, the Nelson."

A grin cracked his face and his coffee brown eyes sparkled. "So, the usual?"

"There are other worthy causes." A defensive tone crept into my voice. There was the debutante ball, a second presentation ball that celebrated the American Royal, Kansas City's famous livestock and horse show, a worthy organization that taught blind children, and a support guild for the hospital.

He held up his hands. "I wasn't judging." He grimaced. "Well, not much. Your friends are incredibly capable. They ought to run corporations, lead not-for-profits, or earn PhDs. Instead, they play bridge and tennis and golf, and give tours at the museum. They've settled into the roles expected of them. They aren't brave like you."

"Me? Brave?"

"You're a successful artist. And you've pursued your art, even when it wasn't comfortable for you."

"You think I'm brave?" A warm glow surrounded my heart.

"I know you are." We resumed walking, and he asked, "Who else will be there?"

"Jill and Tyler Turpin."

"Do I know them?"

"I'm not sure. They live next door to the Clarkes." And Sally had made it clear to me that including them was an obligation. "He's tall, thin, and plays a ton of tennis. She's blonde, petite, and also plays tennis." I didn't add that they never played together. Their marriage couldn't stand the strain. Nor did I tell him that Jill could be a bit catty. And by *bit*, I meant a hissing feline with fully extended claws. Really, she had no reason to be so horrid. As far as I could tell, her life was charmed. She'd graduated high school, gone to Wellesley, come home with a degree in English, married her high school sweetheart, and had children. Granted, Tyler wasn't perfect, but he was a good provider. Jill lived in a beautiful home, belonged to a country club, sent her children to private schools, and was reported to have a generous allowance. That description sounded an awful lot like my first marriage. I'd had those things, and I'd been miserable. Maybe I shouldn't be so quick to judge. "Also, Julie and Robbie Smart."

He frowned. "Are they in the neighborhood?"

"Not really. Leawood. But they're great fun. Julie has never met a stranger. Robbie has a refined palate. A private dinner prepared by Chef Ethan is a treat for him."

"Chef Ethan?"

"Ethan Howe. He has several restaurants in town and occasionally caters small dinner parties. Sally feels awful hosting a party next to what's left of the Dixons' house, but she booked Chef Ethan months ago."

"Did Sally or Ward hear the Dixons fight?" asked Anarchy. Aggie had spent thirty minutes on the phone telling him everything Florence told her. Presumably he'd also called Florence to get the story from the horse's mouth.

"If so, Sally hasn't mentioned it." We climbed the front steps, and I rested my hand on Anarchy's arm, stopping him before he rang the bell. "I should warn you, Jinx and George will be here. She'll question you about the investigation. She can't help herself. She knows there was a body. She wants to know whose."

"I'd like to know that, too." Anarchy rang the bell.

Our hostess opened the door with a martini her hand and a welcoming smile on her face. "Ellison. Anarchy." She blinked four times. "I'm so pleased you're here. I worried Anarchy might not be able—" she hiccupped "—to come. What with the fire…"

Anarchy and I exchanged a quick glance. The martini in Sally's hand wasn't her first.

"I've been looking forward to this all week." Anarchy's lie

was so smooth I almost believed him, and I was the one who'd had to call his office and remind him of our plans.

"Come in, come in." She waved us into the foyer.

We crossed the threshold, and I offered Sally a bakery box tied with a pretty silk ribbon.

"Is this what I think it is?" She rested her martini on a nearby table, made short work of the bow, and peeked in the box.

"Aggie baked." And I'd brought a selection of her cookies as a hostess gift.

Sally bounced on her toes. "Don't tell Ward."

"Pardon?"

"The last time you brought us Aggie's cookies, he ate every single cookie. I was left with crumbs." She clutched the box to her chest. "I'm hiding these. Please—" she nodded toward her living room "—make yourselves at home."

She left us, and Anarchy and I followed her directions into the living room.

Sally and Ward had decorated their home with chintz, English antiques, Oriental carpets, and bland landscapes. It reminded me of Mother and Daddy's house.

Ward waved at us from his spot near the bar. "Welcome. What will you have to drink?"

"A Tom Collins," I replied.

Ward nodded. "For you, Anarchy?"

"A beer, please."

Ward prepared our drinks, looked around his living room, and frowned. "Where did Sally disappear to?"

"Something in the kitchen," I replied.

He grunted. "We hired a chef, and he's made it clear he doesn't want her underfoot."

I wasn't about to tell him his wife was hiding cookies.

A moment later, martini glass in hand, Sally joined us.

"Darling, you promised you'd stay out of the kitchen," said Ward.

"I won't go back. I promise." Sally made an "x" over her heart.

The doorbell rang.

"Excuse me," said Ward. "It's my turn to get the door."

A moment later, Jinx and her husband George appeared at the entrance to the living room.

"Sally." Jinx breezed into the room. "We drove by the Dixons' on our way here. Were you absolutely terrified the fire might spread to your house?"

"I was," Sally replied. "Drink?"

"Club soda with lime, please." Jinx spotted Anarchy. "What have you learned?"

The doorbell rang, and Sally disappeared into the front hall.

Anarchy took a sip of his beer. "It's an active investigation."

Jinx frowned. "Meaning you won't tell me."

"Active investigation," he repeated.

"But the body?" Jinx's question had everyone's full attention.

"We're waiting on identification."

"But there was only one body."

Anarchy offered her a flat look.

Which Jinx ignored. "So, did Marian kill Leonard, or did Leonard kill Marian?"

I schooled my features into a blank mask. Because, if Jinx was right, it sure seemed likely that Marian had committed murder. "What is chef serving tonight?" My clumsy attempt to change the subject made Anarchy's lips twitch, but Ward embraced the question.

"A melon salad for the first course," he replied. "Then grilled lobster Pernod. There's a baked Alaska for dessert."

"I adore lobster Pernod." Jinx lit a cigarette and blew a plume of smoke at the ceiling. "Let's get back to the fire. Were Leonard and Marian having any problems?"

A woman snickered. "Marian is nothing but a problem." Jill had entered the living room without my noticing.

I completely agreed with her assessment, but I'd never express it in public. *If you can't say anything nice, say nothing at all.*

Jill took in our blank faces and huffed. "She's petty and a busybody and as nutty as a fruitcake."

And Mother's spy. I kept that thought to myself.

"No one would blame Leonard if he knocked her off."

"Very few people approve of murder." Anarchy's mild voice hid a steely certainty. Murder was wrong and killers should be punished.

And the body belonged to a man, which made Marian a suspect.

Anarchy's eyes, coffee brown and brimming with intelligence, focused on Jinx. "When you say 'problems,' what do you mean?"

For a moment I thought Jinx might tell him that hers was an ongoing investigation, but she took another puff on her cigarette and said, "Leonard consulted an attorney."

"No!" Sally exclaimed. "Who?"

"Mitchell Gillespie," Jinx replied.

Sally sipped. Slowly. As if considering her next words. "He's a divorce attorney."

"I'm aware." With her love of fresh gossip, it was possible Jinx had a spy in his office.

"Did you ever hear Marian and Leonard argue?" Anarchy asked Sally.

Long seconds passed, then Sally nodded. "Once or twice. This spring, before we turned on the air-conditioner. When the windows were open."

"About what?" Jinx demanded.

"Marian was sure Leonard had someone on the side."

That confirmed what Florence had heard. Marian was missing, and the remains of her house had revealed a dead man. She sure looked guilty.

"Does Marian have family around here?" I asked.

"She has a sister," said Sally. "I believe she lives in Peculiar."

"It's a town south of here," I whispered to my husband.

"Do you know her name?" he asked.

Sally's face scrunched. "Nancy? Nan? Nanette? No, that's not it. I don't remember." She took another sip of her martini. "I'll think of it at three in the morning."

Given the amount of gin she was drinking, I doubted her early morning memory.

"If you do, please let me know." Anarchy was more optimistic than I. About most things. Which was ironic. One would think the homicide detective would hold a jaundiced view of the world. Not him. And one would think a painter of pretty art would wear rose-colored glasses. Not me. I'd found one too many bodies.

So, in my estimation, Marian looked increasingly guilty, Sally would never remember that name, and Jinx would dine out on this conversation for the next month.

CHAPTER FIVE

The soles of my sneakers hit the path at regular intervals, and I focused on my breathing. The already warm morning air pooled uncomfortably in my lungs.

Given the humidity during the summer months, I much preferred swimming to running.

Unfortunately, Max did not agree. He didn't like getting wet. At all. He tugged on his leash, urging me to increase my pace.

"Nope," I told him. I averaged a ten-minute mile and had no desire to run faster.

It was too early for the park to be truly busy. The kids with baseballs or Frisbees, mothers with kids who needed to burn off energy on the playground, and pre-teens who loitered at the picnic tables would appear later. For now, the park belonged to runners and people walking their dogs.

I came up behind a woman moving at a slow jog. "On your left," I warned.

She edged right. "Ellison?" Olive Rhoades' face was flushed a deep red and her tee-shirt clung to her body. "How often do you do this?" Her voice was thready, as if air was a problem.

"Three or four times a week." I matched my pace to hers, and

Max cast an annoyed glance over his shoulder. This barely jogging pace was much too slow for him.

"Does it get any easier?" she gasped.

"Yes."

"I hit the change." Was that a chuckle or a death rattle coming from her heaving chest? "I guess I should say the change hit me. I'm struggling to maintain my weight. And Quinn has no sympathy. The man can eat and drink the same as always. Me? I sniff a single slice of cheesecake, and I gain five pounds."

Olive did more than sniff cheesecake, but I made a sympathetic noise.

"I considered diet pills, but one hears such mixed reviews."

Women died. "You're better off with watching your calories and increasing your exercise."

She harrumphed. "That's what Quinn says, but I've done that. Just wait. Give it ten or fifteen years, then you'll be in my shoes."

How was I supposed to answer that? We rounded the park's corner onto Summit Street and lost the shade. The temperature in the sun seemed ten degrees hotter.

Olive wiped her brow. "Although your mother has maintained her weight. How did she do it?"

"You'll have to ask her."

"I shouldn't say this, but your mother scares me."

"You're not alone." Mother terrified lots of people. Including me.

We shared a brief smile, then Olive stumbled.

I caught her elbow and saved her from falling. "Are you okay?"

"Winded. I need to walk." Olive drew an audible breath.

Max tugged on his leash. He'd been promised a run, not a walk.

"I was planning on calling you this morning."

"Oh?" I glanced at Olive. Her cheeks were tomato red and sweat trickled down the side of her face.

"Florence told Aggie about the Dixons' argument."

"She did."

A squirrel with a death wish skittered across the path, and Max lunged.

The leash flew out of my hand, and the race was on. The squirrel dashed for the nearest tree with Max hot on his tail.

The closest tree was ten feet away.

"Max!" I didn't fancy prying a squirrel out of his jaws. "No!"

He ignored me and ran faster.

The squirrel leapt at the tree and scurried up the trunk.

Max stood at the base with a wide grin on his doggy face. That had been fun, and he'd almost succeeded. He scanned the park for another unsuspecting squirrel.

"Bad dog." I grabbed his leash and pulled him back to the path.

Olive hadn't moved while I chased my dog. "So much energy." She rubbed her palm across the back of her neck. "About Florence. I don't want your husband to think Quinn and I were covering for Marian. We weren't. We would have told what we overheard."

"Was that the only time you heard them argue?"

"Heavens, no. There was one time Marian screeched so loud she sounded like one of those owls she's so crazy about." Marian's collection of owls—everything from macramé, to figurines, to needlepoint pillows—had burned.

"Did you hear what they were fighting about?" I jogged in place.

"The same thing as always—another woman." Her gaze shifted away from me, and I wondered if she might be lying. I also wondered how Leonard managed to attract one woman, much less two.

Max tugged. Hard.

"Olive, I need to run Max. May I have Anarchy call you?"

"I was hoping we could talk. I'd rather not…" She flushed a deeper shade of red. "I'd rather not talk to the police."

"I'll check with Anarchy and call you."

"Thank you, Ellison."

Grace and I walked onto the pool deck together and immediately parted ways.

My daughter was way too cool to hang out with her mom at the pool. She preferred the gaggle of teenaged girls next to the diving well. They could pretend outrage when a teenaged boy cannon-balled off the high drive and splashed them.

I picked a chaise halfway between the deep and shallow ends, spread a towel, adjusted my sunglasses, and settled in. The sun warmed my skin, and I wished I'd had the foresight to fetch an iced tea before I got comfortable.

A pool bag thunked onto the chaise next to mine, and I opened my eyes.

My best friend Libba wore a sheer kaftan over a black bikini. She regarded me over the rims of her oversized sunglasses. "You didn't call and tell me."

"About?"

"The fire." She moved her pool bag to the concrete and spread out a towel.

"I thought you knew."

"I was at my apartment." Libba spent most nights at my next-door neighbor's house.

"Trouble in paradise?"

"No. Charlie flew to Dallas so his kids didn't have to travel alone." Charlie's ex-wife and children lived in Texas while he'd returned to the city of his birth.

"I see."

Libba stretched out on her chaise. "So, tell me about it. Did Marian kill her husband and start the fire to cover her crime? Or did Leonard kill Marian? No one would blame him. What does Anarchy say?"

I flipped a page in my magazine, the latest *Vogue.* "They have an article about Helen Frankenthaler."

"Who?"

"She's a painter. An abstract expressionist."

"Don't change the subject. Did Marian do it?"

"Mrs. Jones, you have a phone call." The lifeguard who'd called my name sounded vaguely surprised that an adult was receiving a call at the pool. Usually the calls (that never ceased) were for teenagers.

I hurried to the lifeguards' desk and accepted the receiver.

"Two minutes, Mrs. Jones."

I cocked a brow, and the sixteen-year-old boy who'd suggested I limit my phone call to two minutes flushed. "Pool rules," he muttered.

"I'll try to keep it brief." I pressed the receiver to my ear. "Hello."

"Ellison, it's me."

"What's wrong?" I asked my husband.

"Do you know someone named Grant Wycliffe?"

"Yes. Why?"

"Any idea why he'd be in the Dixons' house?" Did Anarchy mean the body was Grant's?

I glanced at the openly eavesdropping lifeguard.

"Can we talk at home? I can't tie up this line."

"When will you be home?"

"I planned on staying a few hours, but if you need me, I can—"

"See you at home at four o'clock?" he suggested.

That would give me several hours to relax in the sun. Or fret about Grant. "I can come now."

"I'm tied up right now. I'll see you at four. Love you."

I glanced at the nosy lifeguard. "Love you, too."

A breeze carrying the scent of suntan lotion and chlorine tickled my shoulder blades,. In the baby pool, a brown-as-a-nut, blonde toddler with her hair in pigtails splashed her mother then let loose a high-pitched, delighted laugh. I smiled at the little girl, then leaned over the desk to hang up the receiver. "Thank you," I told the lifeguard.

The phone rang immediately.

The lifeguard rolled his eyes and pressed the receiver to his ear. "Repeat that." Then he spoke into a microphone. "Phone call for Grace Russell. Grace Russell, you have a phone call."

I scanned the pool deck and spotted Grace trotting toward the lifeguard desk. She would not appreciate my listening to her call.

I walked back to my chaise. Why would Grant Wycliff be at the Dixons'? And if the body they'd found belonged to Grant, where were the Dixons? Had they killed Grant?

"Who was on the phone?" Libba's body glistened with tanning oil.

"Anarchy."

Her brows arched. High. So high they practically skimmed her hairline.

I sat. "Do you remember Grant Wycliff?"

Her forehead creased. "I haven't heard that name in years. Why?"

"Anarchy asked about him."

She sat up and stared at me through her dark glasses. "Was it Grant's body in the Dixons' house?"

"Shh."

She took off her sunglasses to gape at me. "Are you sure? Was Grant murdered?"

I glanced around us—anyone could be eavesdropping. "Please, be quiet."

"Fine." She lowered her voice to an actual whisper. "Where are the Dixons?"

"Vacation."

She wrinkled her nose. "Or they killed him and went on the lam."

I frowned at her as if I hadn't wondered the same thing. "Why would Marian and Leonard kill Grant? Grant doesn't even live here."

"That's for Anarchy to figure out."

"Last I heard, Grant lived in Boston. Why was he in Kansas City?"

"Mom?" Grace waited for my attention at the end of the chaise. "Is everything okay?"

"Yes. Why?"

"You got a call." And moms never got calls. Not at the pool. She planted her hands on her hips and looked down at me. "Was it Anarchy? Is everything okay?"

"Yes."

She pursed her lips, a trick she'd learned from her grandmother. "Then why did he call?"

Now was neither the time nor the place to have a group discussion about Anarchy's case. "Who called you?"

She froze.

"So, a boy. Which one?"

"Moooom." She communicated annoyance and my total lack of coolness with a single, long syllable.

"Hi, Mrs. Jones." Debbie, one of Grace's friends, joined her at the end of my chaise. "Grace told me about the fire. I'm so glad Detective Jones is okay."

Grace had told her friends about Anarchy's heroics? I forced a smile. "We all are."

"It's like totally scary," Debbie continued. "Do they know what caused the fire? My Mom says Mrs. Dixon probably fell asleep with a cigarette."

If that were true, the investigators would have found a woman's body in the ashes, not a man's.

Was Grant Wycliff really dead?

For a moment, I was transported back to my teenage years when I was Grace's age, when I was crazy about Grant. He was handsome and fun and my ideal boyfriend, right up to the moment he kissed my sister.

Even as a teenager, Marjorie had possessed a zest for living. As the oldest child, she was supposed to be the rule follower. As the youngest, I was supposed to be the rebel. Instead, Marjorie did whatever she wanted, and, up until last summer, I'd spent my life following the rules. Following those rules got me a fabulous daughter, a beautiful home and a miserable first marriage.

"Mrs. Jones?"

"Sorry. I was wool-gathering. They're not yet sure how the fire started. What are you girls doing tonight?"

The two exchanged a furtive glance. The kind of glance that mothers everywhere recognized. The girls were up to no good.

"We're spending the night at Peggy's," Grace replied.

"Sounds fun." Sounded like a lie. I'd find a reason to call Peggy's mother when I got home.

"We're headed over there when we leave the pool."

"Grace, it's your turn to walk Max." He needed at least two walks a day.

Her face fell.

"I took him for a run this morning."

"But, Mom…"

"But nothing."

"I'll walk him twice tomorrow."

"Grace."

"Please? Pretty please with a cherry on top?"

"Twice tomorrow. No excuses."

"Thanks, Mom." She and Debbie hurried away before I could change my mind.

Libba chuckled. "A sleepover at Peggy's? Tell me you don't believe her."

"It's possible."

Libba frowned at a gray cloud that dared block her sun. "Like time travel or diet chocolate that tastes good or hangover-free martinis." Hangover-free martinis? Libba had put some thought into impossible things. "I bet Peggy's mother thinks her daughter is sleeping over at your house."

"Maybe. I'll ask a few questions. It takes digging to get to the whole truth." The same could be said for murder investigations.

CHAPTER SIX

Thanks to the gathering clouds, I arrived home well before four. Max, who wore an it's-time-for-my-afternoon-walk face, met me at the door.

"Fine," I told him. "Let me change."

I traded my swimsuit for shorts and a tee-shirt and my Dr Scholl's for tennies, then grabbed his leash. "Let's go."

Outside, with the humidity pushing ninety percent, the air seemed almost solid. I was grateful Max wanted to walk, not run. We ambled to Loose Park. We'd reached the park's far side when the first raindrop fell.

Max, whose long pink tongue hung from his mouth, scowled over his shoulder. As if I were responsible for the rain.

"Not my fault." We walked faster.

But not fast enough. That first raindrop was quickly joined by a million more.

Water streamed down my face and soaked my clothes. It turned Max's silver gray coat to a dark graphite.

He pulled on his leash as if he wanted to sprint home.

"What's your hurry?" I asked. "We can't get any wetter." And I didn't fancy running on rain-slicked streets.

Thunder rumbled across the sky, and Max tugged harder. Lightning forked across the sky, and my frightened dog nearly yanked my arm out of its socket.

I compromised. We jogged.

"If I fall, I am holding you responsible."

Max didn't care. He just wanted to get out of the rain.

I tripped over a sodden shoelace, careened forward, and lost my grip on Max's leash.

My dog took off like a bat out of hell.

I cursed softly. Hopefully he was headed home. I had trouble catching him on a good day—a day when the stars aligned and fortune smiled upon me. My chances of catching Max during a storm were nonexistent. Especially when the sky was dark as night.

I headed for home. Unlike Max, I didn't race like Secretariat. I trotted. Carefully. My shoes squelching with each step. Lightning lit the sky, and thunder rumbled, loud enough that I felt it in my bones. A gust of wind buffeted my shoulders. Sudden worry tightened my muscles and coiled in my belly. This storm was dangerous, and I was on a block of darkened houses. No one was home to offer me temporary shelter.

Headlights brightened the street, and a sedan pulled to the curb. The driver's door flew open, and a man got out of the car.

"Ellison!" It was Anarchy. He'd come for me.

I exhaled a breath I hadn't realized I was holding.

"Are you all right?" he demanded. His rough voice was more comforting than a warm blanket on a cold night.

"I'm fine," I told him. "Just wet." Soaked to the skin. Frightened. Endlessly grateful he'd come for me.

"When Max came home without you, I worried." Another fork of lightning lit the sky. He grimaced. "Get in the car." He opened the passenger door, and I climbed in.

The vents were blowing cold air, and I shivered in my wet clothes.

Anarchy took his seat behind the wheel. "You went running during a storm?"

"I took Max for a walk when it was cloudy. The storm came as a surprise."

His fingers tightened on the wheel. The man really had worried.

I wrapped my fingers around his forearm. "I'm fine. Just soaked."

His lips thinned as if he were biting back an argument. "Let's get you home and get you dry." He put the car in gear and drove.

"What did you do with Max?" I asked.

"I put him in the laundry room. He wasn't happy about it."

"He'll get over it." Better an unhappy Max than a wet dog lounging on the furniture. "I'm sorry about your seat."

His lips thinned even more. "Don't give it a thought." He reached for the dash and turned on the heat. "You look cold."

"Thank you." The sudden blast of warm air loosened my taut shoulders. "Thank you for coming. To look for me, I mean."

"I'll always come for you."

Rain pelted the car as if the stormy sky held a deep-seated grudge. The wipers couldn't keep up, and Anarchy drove at a snail's pace. Much as I wanted a hot shower and a cup of coffee, I didn't complain. I was grateful to be out of the weather.

A two-minute drive took ten.

When we arrived home, Anarchy parked as close as possible to the front door. "Ready to run?"

"Sure. Although I can't get any wetter."

He turned off the engine, and we dashed to the house.

Unbelievably, I could and did get wetter.

Anarchy opened the door, and I hurried to the kitchen where the water streaming from my body wouldn't damage the floors.

You look as if you need a cup. Concern laced Mr. Coffee's voice.

"I need a pot."

"Sit." Anarchy's hand on my shoulder pushed me onto a stool. "I'll start the coffee."

Given the way my chilled hands shook, I didn't argue. Instead, I watched Anarchy measure coffee grounds and fill Mr. Coffee's reservoir.

Woof!

"Can Max come out?" asked Anarchy.

"If he stays in the kitchen." I didn't fancy a wet dog stretched out on the velvet couches in the living room. And I knew, without question, that a wet Max would make for the most expensive furniture in the house.

Anarchy closed the doors to the front hall and dining room then freed our dog.

Max entered the kitchen with an attitude. How dare we lock him in the laundry room?

"You smell," I told him.

The wet dog odor nearly eclipsed Mr. Coffee's delicious aroma.

"Also, you ran off. You could have been hit by a car."

Max, who was smarter than most drivers, rolled his amber eyes then fixed his gaze on the top of the fridge. All would be forgiven for a biscuit.

Anarchy, who was a big softy, gave him a bone-shaped treat, and Max settled on his mat. "Coffee?"

"Please."

Anarchy filled a mug, put it in front of me, then fetched the cream.

I doctored my coffee, sipped, and sighed.

"Better?"

I was still cold, wet, and slightly traumatized, but coffee did make everything better. "Yes."

"Do you feel up to talking about Grant Wycliff?"

"We grew up together. Dated in high school."

Anarchy nodded, but said nothing, waiting for more.

When I remained quiet, he asked, "For how long?"

"Until he kissed Marjorie."

Anarchy winced.

"Yeah."

"What else?"

"Grant attended Harvard, then stayed on the East coast. I've heard he occasionally visits his mother. She's not well."

"Is there a reason he'd be in the Dixons' house?"

"He grew up there. Before it belonged to the Dixons, it belonged to the Wycliffs."

"Was he searching for something?"

I grinned into my coffee. "Like a lost will or a family heirloom? Doubtful. The Dixons have lived there forever. And Marian remodeled the house when they moved in."

"So, why was he there?"

I searched for a plausible reason and came up with nothing.

Anarchy, whose wet jeans were molded to his legs, leaned against the counter and crossed his arms over his chest. "Did Wycliff see anyone besides his mother when he came to town?"

I dragged my gaze away from the damp tee shirt struggling to cover Anarchy's chest and replied, "Maybe. Grant and Whit were inseparable in high school."

"Whit?"

"Whit Riley. He and his wife, Tippy, live behind the Rhoades."

"So you went to high school with Whit, too?"

"I went to a girls' school. They went to a boys' school. But, for all intents and purposes, yes."

Anarchy rubbed the back of his neck. "Where can I find Grant's mother?"

"Pleasant Lane."

His brows rose in question.

"It's a nursing home. Mary Wycliff has memory issues."

"Meaning?"

"She remembers thirty years ago like yesterday but can't remember what she had for breakfast."

"Would she talk to me?"

"I'm not sure."

"Would she talk to you?"

"Probably." Grant's mother had seemed to like me when I dated her son.

"Would you go with me to talk to her?"

"You're sure it was Grant's body?"

"We found his wallet and requested dental records from the Boston police department. They'll check with his dentist."

"Boston makes sense. He married a Brahmin."

"Are they still married?"

"We should check with Jinx, but I'm fairly certain they divorced." A vague memory lurked in my brain—a woman who told me Grant's marriage had ended. As if I'd care. I'd had problems with my own marriage at that point. I hadn't possessed the emotional capacity to concern myself with someone else's.

"How long ago?"

"Honestly? I haven't a clue."

Pleasant Lane's halls smelled like antiseptic and stale urine, and I wrinkled my nose.

Anarchy's fingers tightened around my left hand. I used my right to carry a potted plant for Mary.

"Are you going to tell her?" I whispered. "About Grant, I mean."

"Not until we're sure it's him."

The nurse's aide who led us to Mary's room paused next to a closed door. "Mrs. Wycliff will be so pleased to have company."

"How long since Grant visited?" I asked.

Her brow creased. "He was here for Mothers' Day."

Anarchy's gaze settled on her, and she smoothed her uniform as a rosy hue colored her cheeks. "Mrs. Wycliff has friends who visit on Wednesday afternoons. Those are her best days. Mrs. Minton comes on Sunday and Thursday afternoons."

"Mrs. Minton?" I asked.

"Her daughter."

"Of course." I'd completely forgotten Virginia, who was ten years older than Grant and out of the house when we were in high school.

The nurse frowned at us. "Have you known Mrs. Wycliff long?"

"Since I was in high school. I dated her son."

"Oh, good." Her expression smoothed. "The longer she's known someone, the more likely she'll remember them." She knocked gently. "Miss Mary, you have visitors."

Mary Wycliff wore a seersucker housecoat and bedroom slippers. Her white hair looked like cotton candy atop her head, and she held an upside-down book in her hands. She sat in a Naugahyde recliner angled to give her a view of the lawn. Not that the view was particularly nice. Rain continued to fall from a dense gray sky.

She stared at me for long seconds, then said, "Ellison."

"Mrs. Wycliff, it's nice to see you." I deposited the bright pink begonia I carried on a table near the window. "This is for you."

"Thank you, dear. Are you here to see Grant?"

"I'm here to see you."

"How nice." She waved at an empty chair.

"How's Grant? Have you talked to him lately?"

Her brow furrowed. "Just the other day." Her gaze caught on Anarchy. "Who is this?"

"This is my friend, Anarchy."

"Anarchy? What kind of name is that?"

"One I can't forgive my parents for." Anarchy's tone was gentle, almost teasing.

Mary cackled. "I bet. The Leers in Wichita named their daughter Crystal Chanda. And there are the Hoggs in Texas. They named their daughter Ima. But I believe Anarchy might be worse. You can't marry out of it."

"If only you'd been there when my parents were picking names."

"I'd have set them straight." She stared at my husband. "You look like Steve McQueen, except his eyes are blue. Yours are brown. How do you know Ellison? You do realize she's dating my son?"

"We met at the pool," I told her. "Grant lives in Boston now."

Her eyes clouded. "That's right. He married that woman. Olivia." The way she pronounced each syllable told me what she thought of Grant's ex-wife. "They have children. Two boys." Her tone softened. "Oliver and Baxter."

"What did—does Grant do in Boston?"

Mary didn't seem to notice my slip. "Something with securities. He got an MBA at Harvard, you know."

"I remember. Very impressive," I assured her. "What did you and Grant talk about the last time you spoke?"

"Ellison, you can't hold this against him. It was your sister's fault." Mary had wandered back in time.

"I'm sure you're right." Marjorie had made a game of kissing my high school boyfriends. But no one made them kiss her back. They did that on their own. Even Grant.

"He was worried," said Mary.

"About what?" Anarchy asked.

"Someone lied to him."

I leaned forward. "Who?"

"He didn't say. That sister of yours is no better than she should be, but Frances refuses to see it." Mary had that right. Marjorie could do no wrong until she married a man who manufactured condoms. Mother still hadn't entirely forgiven her for that. It didn't help that Marjorie had come home from college, saying that her boyfriend from Ohio was in the rubber business. Mother had assumed tires. That Greg manufactured the King Cobra condom came as an unpleasant shock.

"What else did Grant say?"

"He has two sons. Handsome boys."

"I'm sure."

"Is he taking you to prom?"

I cast a quick glance at Anarchy's face.

"To the junior prom, yes."

"You could do worse."

I'd done much better. I smiled at my husband.

"You and Grant and Tippy and Whit are so dashing together. I'm sure you'll be close friends forever."

It hadn't worked out like that. "The person who lied to Grant, do you know who it is?"

She frowned at the begonia. "Who lied to Grant?"

We were getting nowhere.

I patted her hand. "Mother sends her regards."

"Frances can be terrifying."

Amen, sister. "Yes, she can."

"She can also be blind." Mary nodded, as if agreeing with someone who was invisible to Anarchy and me. "When it comes to family, we see what we want to see."

A chill trickled down my spine. Did she mean Marjorie or someone else?

CHAPTER SEVEN

I stared out the kitchen window and sighed. "I was supposed to play golf with Daddy this afternoon." Usually on Sundays, Daddy played with his cronies, men he had decades of history with. His invitation for me to join him on the course had come as a pleasant surprise.

Mr. Coffee made a sympathetic sound.

"The rain isn't letting up." After last night's thunderstorm, rain had fallen in steady sheets for hours. And hours. "Even if it clears, it'll be cart path only." The greenskeeper wouldn't want golf carts on his sodden fairways. "Daddy will cancel." My father had reached an age where carrying his bag or using a pushcart had lost its appeal.

Brnng, brnng.

"I bet that's him." I picked up the receiver. "Jones' residence."

"Ellison, it's me." Daddy sounded regretful. "I hate to do this, but the rain—"

"How about next weekend? Maybe Anarchy can join us."

"It's a date. Has Anarchy learned anything more about the fire?"

Max, who desperately needed exercise, trotted into the

kitchen with a throw pillow in his mouth. And not just any throw pillow. One Mother had needle-pointed for me. The expression in his amber eyes said I'd have to chase him to get it back.

"No!"

"Pardon?"

"Sorry, Daddy. Max is being naughty." Such an understatement. I gave my dog the evil eye.

Max could not have cared less about my scowl.

"Nothing new there," said my father. "You could have adopted a lab or a Golden retriever."

"That ship has sailed. He has the pillow Mother made for me."

Daddy barked a short laugh. "I promise not to tell your mother. It's a good thing he's handsome."

Very handsome. But there was more to Max than good looks and dubious behavior. "He's also brave."

Daddy huffed as if he weren't yet convinced that Max possessed the heart of a lion. "I'll let you deal with the menace."

I hung up the phone and reached for the treat container atop the fridge. "I'll trade you."

Max's tail wagged.

I held the biscuit just out of my dog's reach. "Drop the pillow."

He eyed the treat, considered the trade, then dropped his prize onto the floor.

I handed over the biscuit and reclaimed the pillow.

With a pleasure-doing-business-with-you swagger, Max headed for his mat.

"Don't do this again, Max."

He made no promises.

The back door opened and Grace hurried into the kitchen, shedding raindrops hither and yon. Her clothes were wrinkled, her hair tangled, and her skin pale.

If I didn't know for a fact that she'd spent the night at Peggy's house, I'd have assumed the worst. "How was the sleepover?"

"We stayed up and watched the late movie." I very much doubted that was the original plan, but the rain had put a damper on their schemes. Lavender half-moons hung beneath Grace's eyes. Either they'd stayed up much later than the late movie or something was wrong.

"Everything okay?"

Her eyes narrowed. "You called Peggy's mother."

Guilty as charged. "I did." And I had no remorse.

"To check up on me. You don't trust me." Her voice rang with righteous indignation.

"It's easy to make a bad decision."

"That's ridiculous. I'm a model child."

"You are. But even the best kids make missteps." A certain out-of-control party came to mind.

"Debbie's mom didn't call." She made it sound as if Debbie's mother was a paragon of good parenting. She wasn't.

"Looking to trade me in?"

"No. But you should trust me."

"I do. It's your friends I don't trust."

Her mouth opened and shut without forming actual words. She had no comeback for my excellent point, so she crossed her arms and scowled. She couldn't argue. If—when—Grace got into trouble, one of her friends usually had a hand in it. "I still think you should give me the benefit of the doubt."

"Keep your nose clean for six months, and we'll talk."

"Fine," she huffed. "How long is it supposed to rain?"

I glanced out the window. "It won't stop anytime soon."

"All night?"

"Yes."

"Tomorrow?"

"Yes."

"Sweet." Her expression lightened. "That means no swim practice. I can sleep in."

It was a universal truth that teenagers hated getting up early for swim practice. Grace would rather have a nine o'clock curfew than drag herself to the pool at half past seven in the morning.

Most mornings I rose before six to swim, so I wasn't exactly sympathetic. "If there's no lightning, they may have you swim."

"In the rain?" She sounded horrified.

"Worried about getting wet?"

"You think you're funny."

"I'm hysterically funny." I really wasn't. "What are you doing today?"

She glanced out the window at the dripping gray. "I'm not sure. Summer reading list? What about you?"

"I'll paint." The light in my third floor studio might be too dim to successfully add color to canvas. "Or sketch."

Grace opened the fridge and surveyed its contents. "What are you working on?"

"A landscape and a still life." Both painted in bold bright hues totally at odds with weather. "Did you have breakfast?"

"Granola. I'm still hungry." With a dissatisfied sigh, Grace closed the refrigerator door and helped herself to an apple from the bowl on the kitchen island. "Where's Anarchy?"

"At work."

Grace bit into the apple. "Does he know who died?"

"He has an idea."

"Who?"

"Active investigation."

"I can keep a secret."

"Not my secret to share."

She stared at me, weighing my words, then gave a brief nod. "I'll ask him."

Max, who'd long since finished his biscuit, stood, stretched, and padded to the back door where he gave a half-hearted scratch.

Grace was closest, and she opened the door, welcoming a cool breeze and the scent of wet grass into the kitchen.

Max gazed through the screen for long seconds, as if the intensity of his stare might stop the rain. When the rain continued to fall, he huffed his disapproval.

"Sorry, buddy." Grace scratched behind his ears.

"You'll have to get him out at some point."

"Me?" She pressed her free hand to her chest. "It's raining."

"I noticed. But you did promise to take him out twice today."

If eye rolls were audible, Grace's would be deafening.

"Not while it's raining." She closed the door and headed toward the back stairs. "I guess I'll read until it clears."

"Grace."

"What?" she snapped.

"There are these wonderful things called umbrellas. People carry them in the rain."

"You're really not funny."

"You're really walking the dog."

She turned her back on me.

"And do not leave the apple core in your room." I could sense another eye roll as she climbed the stairs.

Someday you'll miss this.

Would I?

Mr. Coffee was right. I would miss this. By teenaged standards, Grace really was a model child. I was already dreading the day she left for college.

"I won't miss eye rolls and attitude."

We'll see about that.

I had a sneaking suspicion he was right. Rather than reply, I pulled the Sunday paper from its damp plastic sleeve and scanned the headlines.

Anything about the fire or the murder?

"No. Anarchy seems sure that the body they found belongs to Grant Wycliff." Mr. Coffee was the best at keeping secrets. I could discuss Anarchy's case without worry. He would not repeat a single word.

Not one of the Dixons? Mr. Coffee seemed surprised.

"Nope."

What do you know about Wycliff?

I helped myself to more coffee. "I haven't seen him in years. He's divorced and lives—lived—in Boston. According to his mother, he has two sons, Oliver and Baxter."

Who would want him dead?

"No idea."

Why was he in the Dixons' house?

"No idea."

Who would know?

"His ex-wife? Maybe his sister."

His sister?

"Honestly, I forgot he had one. She married and moved away before Grant and I started dating. She must be back in Kansas City. The aide at Pleasant Lane says she visits her mother twice a week."

They weren't close?

"Not remotely."

Does Wycliff have friends in Kansas City?

"He and Whit Riley were best friends in high school."

What about college?

"Different universities." Also, I had a vague recollection of them falling out.

I hate to be the bearer of bad news, but turn around.

I turned.

Max held a shoe in his mouth.

I scowled at my dog. "Really?"

His tail wagged. This was fun. And rewarding.

"I bought those loafers for Anarchy on our honeymoon." They were Italian and ridiculously expensive.

Max did not care. If anything, the shoe's value made it worth more in a trade.

I reached for the treat jar, and victory gleamed in his eyes. Swapping treasures for treats was his new favorite pastime.

We made the exchange.

"I am not playing this game all day."

My dog simply grinned. We'd see about that.

"Thank heavens the rain stopped." It was three o'clock and Anarchy, who'd finished work for the day, and I were walking Max. Not Grace. She'd conveniently left for Kimberly's house a mere ten minutes before the rain let up. I was pretty sure that counted as a parenting failure. Rather than dwell on my shortcomings, I focused on my dog's. "Max has been driving me nuts."

"Cabin fever."

Max danced around a puddle on the sidewalk then pulled me through it.

"Let me." Anarchy took the leash.

"I'm glad you're home."

"Me. Too." His free hand claimed mine. "We're still waiting on the autopsy report from the medical examiner and the dental records from Boston. The Boston PD did visit Wycliff's ex-wife. She claims she hasn't seen him in months."

"Are you positive it's Grant?"

"Not one hundred percent. But it's not Dixon. The corpse was the wrong size."

I shuddered. "Okay. But why Grant?"

"We found his wallet in the yard."

"The yard? What was it doing in the yard?"

"Your guess is as good as mine. It's our best clue to the body."

Woof.

Max, who'd spotted Whit Riley and his Airedale, Finnegan, pulled against Anarchy's hold.

"It's okay," I told my husband. "They're buddies." The two dogs had played together as puppies and still got along.

Finn wagged his tail so hard his whole body shook. He dragged Whit toward us.

"Nice that the rain took a break." Whit wore a bright red wind-breaker decorated with a tiny crocodile, a light blue polo shirt, khaki shorts, and yellow galoshes. A strong breeze tugged at his thinning hair and sprinkled all of us with raindrops still clinging to the trees.

"It is," I agreed. "Max definitely needed a walk." I'd negoti-ated so many trades with my bored dog that running out of biscuits was a real possibility.

Max and Finn sniffed each other's anatomy. Then Finn lowered onto his front legs and yipped. Max danced around his friend, ready to romp through the wet grass.

"If I bring Finn back muddy, Tippy will kill me."

"I understand. Muddy paws. Clean floors." I glanced at Anar-chy. Like Whit, his attention was on the happy dogs. I swal-lowed sudden nerves, gathered my courage, and said, "I visited Mary Wycliff yesterday."

Anarchy stiffened.

Whit tilted his head and shifted his focus to me. "Did she know you?"

"Yes, but she thought I was a teenager."

Whit frowned, and there was genuine sadness in his eyes. "I should go see her. Poor woman. Grant comes when he can."

"The aide said he came for Mother's Day. Do the two of you stay in touch?"

"We had drinks when he came into town last summer. He

pitched a business deal, then talked about his divorce. Contentious. Olivia was sure he'd been unfaithful."

"He told you that?"

"Not exactly." Whit flushed nearly as red as his jacket. "Olivia called us last spring. Except, she didn't know it was us. She was going through Grant's address book. I guess he uses initials rather than names. She called every number in his book."

She'd been looking for the other woman.

Wow. My first husband had cheated, but I would no more have called the numbers in his address book than fly to the moon on one wing. Maybe I'd had too much pride. Maybe I hadn't cared enough about him or our marriage, which we'd maintained for Grace's sake. "She must have been terribly upset."

"Beside herself." He winced. "I was a groomsman in their wedding. I always figured they'd be together forever."

"Did she find the woman?" asked Anarchy.

Whit's light blue eyes took in the man still holding my hand.

Anarchy wore faded jeans, old tennis shoes, and a police-issue rain jacket.

Whit's lip curled as if he were fighting a sneer. "You'd have to ask her."

I tamped down a flash of annoyance. Whit had no reason—not one—to feel superior to my husband. Anarchy was a hero. Whit was not.

"I'll do that." Anarchy's voice was mild, as if Whit's misplaced sense of superiority amused him.

"Did you invest?"

Whit stared at me as if he didn't understand the question.

"In Grant's deal. Did you invest?"

"No. I passed."

I manufactured a smile. "Whatever happened to Grant's sister? Virginia?"

"She and her husband moved back here a few years ago. From some place in California."

"Really? I haven't run into her."

"You wouldn't." Another tiny, superior sneer twisted Whit's face. "They don't run in our crowd. Bob had a few financial setbacks. I think Virginia spends her time taking care of Mary. It takes the pressure off Grant."

"I'm sure Mary appreciates that. Grant, too." The aide had said Virginia visited her mother twice a week. Two afternoons. That hardly counted as taking care of Mary.

"They live over in Raytown."

"The woman who does Max's nails lives over there."

Both men stared at me.

Anarchy released my hand and wiped a droplet of water from his forehead. "You have Max's nails done?"

"I'm afraid to cut them. Inez trims his nails and gives him a bath, and he comes home certain that he's the most gorgeous creature in the universe. In fact, I should probably call her. After all this rain, he'll need a bath."

"You'll have to share the woman's number with Tippy." Whit tugged on Finn's leash. "I should probably get this guy some more exercise. He's been climbing the walls."

Whit and his dog went one way.

We went the other.

When we were out of hearing distance, Anarchy asked, "Do the Wycliffs have money?"

"Yes." I searched my memories for the source of their wealth and came up empty. Probably, but, as a teenage girl, I'd cared more about Grant's blue eyes and easy smile than his father's net worth. "I'm surprised Virginia is in Raytown."

"Why?"

"It's a long way from here." I waved at the houses on our block. All enormous. All settled on perfectly manicured lawns.

"You don't mean miles."

"I do not."

We stopped as Max watered a lawn, and I looked up into Anarchy's handsome face. "Are you thinking Virginia had something to do with Grant's death?"

"I'm thinking I should talk to her. Sooner rather than later."

CHAPTER EIGHT

Jinx arrived on my doorstep at precisely nine o'clock in the morning. I'd called last night and invited her over, because if anyone knew the source and breadth of the Wycliffs' wealth it was her.

I welcomed my friend inside, and she shoved Max away from her crotch before I could scold him. Then she deposited her umbrella in the brass stand near the front door and handed Aggie her raincoat.

Aggie wrapped her free hand around Max's collar and dragged him away.

"I thought we'd have coffee in the living room."

Jinx settled onto a wingback, arched a brow, and said, "Well?"

"Coffee?"

"Please."

I poured from the silver pot into a Spode cup. "Cream or sugar?"

"Cream."

I added a jot of cream to Jinx's cup then handed it to her. "Aggie made coffee cake."

"I can't say no to that."

No one could. Aggie's baking was legendary.

I put a slice on a plate which Jinx immediately claimed. My guest sorted, I poured my own coffee and helped myself to cake.

"This is the best coffee cake I've ever had." Jinx forked another bite.

"I'll tell her you said so." I took a bracing sip of coffee. "Thank you for meeting me this morning."

Her lips twitched. "What do you want, Ellison?"

Inviting Jinx to coffee wasn't something I usually did. Ever did. But Anarchy and I had discussed this. I took a deep breath. "I want to share with you what I know."

Jinx leaned in, going so far as to put down her plate. "Why do I feel as if there's a catch?"

"I'd like to ask you a few questions."

She lifted her left brow. "About?"

"About something I'd prefer you keep to yourself until Anarchy closes the case."

She nodded. Slowly. "Okay. But first, what did you think about the dinner at Sally and Ward's?"

"It was delicious."

"I don't mean the food. Sally was drunk."

"Yes."

"When was the last time you saw Sally drunk?"

I considered her question. "Never."

"Makes me wonder…"

"About?" I asked.

"If she had a grudge against Marian."

I gaped at my friend.

She sat in my favorite wingback chair with her ankles neatly crossed. One look at her navy blue wrap skirt embroidered with bright red ladybugs and her white cotton shirt with a Peter Pan collar and anyone with half a brain would peg her for an upper middle-class lady who lunched, not someone who hinted that her hostess might have committed murder.

"Everyone in the neighborhood had a grudge against Marian."

"Enough to kill her?"

"About that..."

She waited. Expectantly.

"This is something you can't repeat."

She nodded. "Go on."

"The body isn't a Dixon."

She sat back in her chair. "Then who is it?"

"There's a good chance it's Grant Wycliff."

"Mary Wycliff's son?"

"Yes."

"Lives in Boston."

"Yes."

"Got divorced last year."

"Yes."

"Cheated on you with your sister?"

I jerked back in my seat. "How do you remember that? It was almost twenty-five years ago."

She shrugged. "I just do."

"Well, yes. That Grant Wycliff."

And why do you and, presumably, Anarchy think Grant's body was in the Dixons' house?"

"There was personal property recovered."

"I see. So the fire had nothing to do with Leonard's affair?"

"It doesn't seem that way." I shifted in my chair. "What can you tell me about Virginia Wycliff Minton?"

"She's ten, maybe eleven, years older than we are, married a man she met in college, and lives in Evanston, Illinois."

"Not anymore."

"Oh?" Her eyes sparkled at the possibility of fresh gossip.

"She's in Kansas City. According to Whit, she lives in Raytown."

"With your dog groomer."

"She doesn't live with my dog groomer."

"You know what I mean." Jinx rubbed her chin. "Why are you asking about Virginia?"

"I'm just trying to figure out why someone would murder Grant."

"And you think his sister did it?"

"Not necessarily. I got the impression he's paying to keep Mary at Pleasant Lane. I doubt his sister would want that to end."

Jinx pulled a face.

"What?" I demanded.

"I doubt Mary needs any help paying for Pleasant Lane. The Wycliff family has oil wells. Lots of them."

"Then why is Virginia living in Raytown?"

Jinx closed her eyes and tapped a perfectly manicured nail against her lips. "Do you mind If I smoke?"

I did. "Do you mind if we sit on the patio?"

"It's raining." She looked at me as if she expected me to change my mind. When I didn't, she sighed. "Smoking helps me think, but never mind. I can wait." She took another bite of cake. "Raytown, huh?"

"Yep."

"Harold Wycliff didn't approve of Virginia's husband. He cut her off. Before Harold died, he put most of his assets in a trust. The trustee is paying for Mary's care, not Grant."

"What happens to the trust when Mary dies?"

"I'm not sure," Jinx admitted.

Under usual circumstances, the trust would be split between the remaining children. If one of the children predeceased their mother, as Grant had, his share would go to his children.

"Do you know the trustee?"

"No, but I can ask around." She lifted her coffee cup to her lips and sipped. "I'll try to find him for you."

I took another bite of Aggie's cake, a cinnamon and butter streusel that could make angels sing. "Thank you."

"If it is Grant's body, how did he get into the Dixons' house?"

"That's a good question. Marian was always so worried about burglary that she locked the place tight as a drum." She'd worried a dastardly owl collector might steal her precious (to her) figurines.

Jinx's gaze shifted to the front windows and their view of the wreckage across the street. "Someone could have broken in."

If so, we'd never know. Not when every door, every pane of glass, and most of the walls were destroyed.

"Why did you hint that Sally burned down the Dixons' house?"

"Leonard was having an affair."

"You can't mean with Sally." Sally took care of herself. She had a trim figure, auburn hair that she wore in a flattering page-boy style, and a pretty face. Leonard had softened with age, sported a receding hairline, and often wore a beleaguered expression that probably came from spending decades listening to Marian. "If Sally cheated on Ward, wouldn't she pick a better looking man?" Except that wasn't how cheating worked. My first husband had cheated on me with Prudence Davies, a woman with more than a passing resemblance to a horse. I put Prudence and her horse teeth out of my mind.

"One would think, but Sally is never drunk."

"Maybe she was nervous about the party." My weak excuse had Jinx offering me an indulgent smile, as if I were so naïve she didn't know how to respond.

"She and Ward did not exchange a single word all night."

"They were entertaining guests." Now I sounded desperate, as if Jinx were about to rip the rose-colored glasses clean off my face.

"You're an artist. Aren't you supposed to be observant?"

I tried not to observe my friends. Of course, I'd noticed that Sally was half-sloshed. Okay, fully sloshed. Of course, I'd noticed the tension between her and Ward. She'd hidden cookies. From her husband. He'd openly criticized his wife. That didn't mean Sally was having an affair. I said as much.

Jinx brought two fingers to her lips as if they held a cigarette. "For as many bodies as you find, one would think you'd take a more realistic view of the world."

She meant a more cynical view. I refused to be cynical about my friends.

Max wandered into the living room and eyed the cake on the coffee table.

"Don't even think about it," I warned him.

He wagged his stubby tail and grinned as if stealing (and inhaling) Aggie's cake had never occurred to him. Call me cynical, I was not fooled.

"May I offer you another slice?" I asked.

"I'd love to, but I can't." She patted her flat stomach.

"Would you please excuse me for a moment?" I picked up the cake plate, headed for the kitchen, and deposited the cake in a spot where a moment's inattention wouldn't result in a dog with a belly ache.

When I returned to the living room, Max was licking the crumbs off Jinx's plate.

"He's hard to resist," she said. "Those eyes."

She should try harder.

"A real charmer." My voice was flat.

We chatted another twenty minutes, covering Libba and Charlie and just how serious they were, how much we both disliked Jill Turpin, and Tippy Riley's inability to see if a tennis ball landed in or out. Jinx had strong opinions about that one. Then Jinx gathered her handbag and stood. "I should get going."

"Thank you for coming."

"Thank you for the coffee and cake. I'll see what I can find out about the trust."

"I appreciate that."

"You'll keep me updated about the investigation?"

"As much as I'm able."

She nodded, and I walked her to the front door where we both gazed out at the drippy morning.

She collected her umbrella. "I'm so sick of rain. My tennis game has been cancelled."

"I haven't been able to swim." I flashed her a smile. "Oh, to have our problems."

"We are lucky."

We exchanged a quick hug. "Have a good day. I'll see you soon."

She hurried to her car, and I returned to the living room to collect the coffee cups and licked-clean plates which I returned to the kitchen.

Aggie looked up from her perusal of a cookbook. "I would have picked those up."

"It was no trouble. Your cake was fabulous. Jinx said it was the best she'd ever had."

"I'm glad she enjoyed it."

I put the dirty dishes on the counter and asked, "How often do you talk to Florence?"

She stood and took the dishes to the sink. "Why?"

I clenched my hands, hating what I was about to ask. "Has she ever heard the Clarkes argue?" The words came out in a rush.

Aggie tilted her head, considering the question. She turned on the faucet and began rinsing the dishes. "Is this about the murder?"

With Jinx sitting across from me, I'd been convinced of Sally's innocence. But the Clarkes lived behind the Dixons. It would be laughably easy for Sally or Ward to cut across their back yards and…and what? Not for one second did I believe that Sally would take up with Leonard, but she or Ward might have had a reason to kill Grant. What that reason might be, I couldn't imagine. "Maybe."

She nodded. "I'll find out the next time I see her."

Anarchy plopped next to me on the couch in the family room.

I turned toward him and smiled. "You're home early."

He nodded at the television where Janie from Milgram's enumerated the grocery store's weekly specials. "What are you watching?"

"The local news. I'm waiting for the weather report. How was your day?"

He glanced at his watch. "It's after five. May I pour you a drink?"

"That bad?" I offered him a sympathetic face. "Did you hear from Boston?"

He stood. "What'll you have?"

"A gin and tonic."

Anarchy fixed our drinks then returned to his spot on the couch. We clinked glasses, and I said, "Well?"

"It's Wycliff."

"Did you find his sister?"

"I left a message on her machine."

"Is the autopsy back?"

Anarchy leaned back far enough that his chin tilted toward the ceiling. "No cause of death yet."

"But?" Something was bothering him. I could tell.

"There was no smoke in his lungs. He was dead before the fire started."

I let that sink in.

He leaned forward, lowering his head and resting his elbows on his knees. "We need to find the Dixons."

"Hold that thought."

Cheryl, the weather girl, pointed at a map. "Continued rain in the forecast. We won't see the sun until Wednesday."

Oh, joy. Just in time for another swim meet.

She turned to a three-quarters angle. "Expect cool temperatures."

Anarchy's gaze fixed on the screen. "Have you ever wondered why there are weather men, but women who give weather reports are weather girls?"

I was fairly certain Cheryl lacked a meteorology degree. She brought other double D assets to the broadcast.

"Very sexist," I agreed. "Think about the cop shows —*Columbo, Kojak, Baretta, Banacek, The Rockford Files, Starsky and Hutch, Barney Miller, McCloud, Mannix.*" If I thought hard enough, I could probably add to the list. "All men's names."

"There's *McMillan and Wife.*"

That earned him an eye roll. "You're making my case for me. One show with a female lead. One. And it's called *Police Woman.*"

"At least it's not *Police Girl.*"

"True." I took a sip of my drink.

"Did you talk to Jinx? What did she say?"

"The Wycliffs have oil money. A trust is paying Mary's bills."

Anarchy frowned. "So why is Virginia living in Raytown?"

"Her father cut her off."

"What happened to him?"

"He's been gone five or six years. I think his funeral was the last time I saw Grant."

"If she needed money, especially after the father died, why didn't Mary help her?"

"Maybe she couldn't. If all the assets are in a trust, disbursements might not have been up to her. And now her memory is too muddled to make financial decisions."

"Hopefully Virginia calls back."

"If she doesn't, you know where to find her."

His brows rose.

"Two afternoons a week."

"Right." He took a large sip of his beer.

"Jinx thinks she can find the trustee."

"And she can get the terms of the trust?"

"I wouldn't bet against her."

"You have amazing friends." He inched closer to me. "Which is hardly surprising." He took the drink from my hands and put it on the coffee table.

"Oh?" My heart fluttered as he leaned closer.

"Because you're amazing." His lips brushed against mine.

"You think so?"

"I know so." His hand delved into my hair and he leaned in for another kiss.

My lips tingled in anticipation, but Anarchy stiffened. Pulled away. "Max!"

I glanced over my shoulder and spotted my very bored, very naughty dog with my new Gucci handbag dangling from his mouth.

"Max!" I was loud enough to alert the neighborhood. Even with the windows closed.

CHAPTER NINE

I sat up out of a dead sleep. My fingers clutched the sheets, and my heart beat double time. "The cat!"

Max stirred at my exclamation.

Anarchy did not.

"Anarchy!" I shook his arm.

"What?" he mumbled.

"The cat."

Max, who was not a fan of felines, growled low in this throat.

"What cat?"

Either my memory or my subconscious supplied the cat's name. "Percival. Marian's cat. The one you saved." The one no one had seen since the fire.

My husband stirred. "What about the cat?"

"Percival was in the house."

"I'm aware. I've got the scratches to prove it."

"Marian cares about her owl collection and that cat. There is no way she would have left Percival without making arrangements for his care."

Anarchy rubbed his eyes, then checked the clock. "It's three in the morning."

"It is," I agreed. "So?"

"Ellison, you're brilliant."

"Thank you."

"Can you be brilliant closer to seven?"

"But the cat."

"You're right. From what we know of Marian, she'd never leave Percival to fend for himself. We'll look into this. But there's nothing we can do right now. Come on." He patted my pillow. "Go back to sleep."

Reluctantly, I lowered my head to the pillow. "Sorry I woke you."

"I'm not. You really are brilliant."

I snuggled against Anarchy's broad chest and drifted back to sleep. I dreamed of an angry Persian cat who blamed me for being left out in the rain. When I opened my eyes shortly before eight, my husband's side of the bed was cold.

"Where is Anarchy?" I asked Max, who still lounged on his cushy bed.

He yawned in answer.

I pulled on a bathrobe and headed for the kitchen where I found Mr. Coffee's pot half-full. Still fresh.

"Thank heavens." I poured a mug then added cream. "And thank you."

You're welcome. Mr. Coffee was always pleasant in the morning. Actually, Mr. Coffee was always pleasant. No qualifier needed. Many people I knew could learn from him.

Max ambled into the kitchen, and I let him out in the backyard.

Anarchy left a note.

"He did? Where?"

To my left.

On the counter, next to Mr. Coffee, I found a few quick lines

*—The cat! You are brilliant. Have gone to the office. I'll call later.
Love, A.*

The smile on my lips was dopey. I didn't care if I looked like a fool in love. I was.

What are you doing today?

I refilled my mug, the first one having gone down too quickly. "Bridge."

With Jinx, Libba, and Daisy?

"Exactly. Maybe one of them will know who Marian used to take care of Percival when she went out of town. Although..."

Although?

I pushed a hank of hair away from my face. "You'd think the pet-sitter would have notified Marian that the house burned down."

Do you think something happened to the Dixons?

"Possibly. I still can't think of a reason Grant would be in their house. Also, chances are good he was murdered there."

The fire.

"No."

He was dead before the fire? It was hard to surprise Mr. Coffee, but I'd done it.

"Yes."

How?

"The medical examiner hasn't said."

Max scratched on the back door, and I let him in.

He settled on his haunches and stared at the top of the fridge as if his very life depended on keeping the treats in his line of sight.

"You've had a million treats. You're going to get fat," I warned.

In Max's mind, there was no such thing as too many treats. His gaze remained fixed. This—a trip to the backyard, then a biscuit—was part of his morning routine. Sacrosanct. Like not wearing white after Labor Day or turning a knife's blade inward when setting a table.

I glanced outside. A soft mist swaddled the yard, but there was no actual rain. "Fine." I gave Max his biscuit. "But we're going for a run as soon as I get changed."

His tail wagged. He didn't like the wet, but he was sick of being inside.

And I was sick of his trade-your-belongings-for-a-biscuit game. We'd swapped for pens, shoes, purses, a blanket pulled off Grace's bed, Anarchy's badge, my billfold, a copy of *Watership Down*, Grace's diary, and the sweater I'd picked up at Swanson's sale last week.

Our run was damp, but uneventful.

When we got home, I took a long shower then got ready for bridge. I chose a seersucker dress and white sandals and threw a white cardigan over my shoulders. Satisfied with my appearance, I descended the back stairs to the kitchen.

Aggie, who wore a turquoise kaftan fringed with little orange balls, looked up from folding one of Grace's tee-shirts. "Florence is meeting me at Mac's for a glass of wine late this afternoon." Mac was Aggie's boyfriend. He owned a restaurant just east of Brookside that served out-of-this-world Italian food.

"Thank you. You'll let me know what she says?"

"Should I call tonight?" Aggie had a room at our house, but increasingly she spent the night at Mac's. I strongly suspected she'd soon be giving up the room and changing her last name. My prayer was for her to continue working. First, because she was a part of our family. Second, because I didn't see how we'd ever manage without her.

"Don't interrupt your evening with Mac. We can catch up in the morning."

She nodded. "I'll leave chicken salad in the fridge for dinner. There are bagels and croissants, and I'll slice some fruit. Also, there's strawberry ice cream in the freezer."

"Thank you. Sounds perfect." Aggie made fabulous chicken salad. No grapes. No nuts. Just plenty of celery, a sparing amount of mayo, and a hint of tarragon. "Max and I ran five miles. That should take the edge off."

She chuckled at my optimism. "I bought more biscuits when I was at the market. You went through almost a whole box in just a few days."

"He has a new game."

"I know. He stole my leather handbag. The one painted with yellow daisies."

Max, who rested on his mat, followed our conversation carefully, but failed to look remotely repentant.

"If he damaged your handbag, I'll replace it."

"No damage." She eyed him critically. "I imagine the run will help."

"I hope so." I gathered my handbag (white to match my shoes) and car keys. "I'm off."

The lawns I passed on my way to the club were incredibly lush and deeply, verdantly green, and the air was so clean it sparkled. Maybe rain wasn't all bad. I thought of being stuck in a house with Max for another day and decided I preferred sunshine.

Only a handful of cars dotted the parking lot. The cool damp air made it a bad day for swimming, and wet courts and fairways meant tennis and golf were out as well.

I slotted my TR6 into a spot near the entrance and breezed into the clubhouse.

Jinx waited for me in the card room. "I don't know anything about the trustee. Not yet."

"I appreciate your trying."

"Give me another day or two. Anything new in the investigation?"

"It's definitely Grant," I told her. "But please, keep that to yourself."

"Promise."

"What are you two whispering about?" Libba dropped into the seat across from me.

I refused—*refused*—to rehash the murder investigation with Libba. "How are Charlie's kids?"

"The poor man. He didn't count on the rain. He planned on keeping them busy here at the club. The Royals' games have been rained out, and Worlds of Fun is closed. The kids are cooped up in the house. It's been miserable."

"There's always the Nelson," I suggested.

"Charlie does not want to take his kids to an art museum. He wants to be a cool dad."

"Art is cool."

She reached across the table and patted my hand. "Sure it is."

"What have they been doing?"

"Crazy eights. They've been playing crazy eights." From the crazy look in her eyes, she'd been playing with them.

"Shall we draw for deal?" asked Jinx.

I pulled the nine of diamonds.

Jinx drew the six of clubs.

Libba drew the ace of spades. "I guess it's me. Are the cards made?"

"I always like to shuffle a few times." Jinx claimed the white deck with the club's logo in crimson.

I shuffled the red deck with the logo in white. When I was done, I put the deck to my right and watched Libba deal.

"Sorry, sorry." Daisy entered the room as Libba dealt the last card. The late arrival sat across from Jinx and raked her hands through her hair. "Hans' new obsession is socks." Hans was the long-haired dachshund her husband adopted despite Daisy's valid objections that she didn't have time to care for a dog. "He's stolen every sock in the house. And hidden them."

At least Max was trading for our belongings, not squirreling them away. "You can't find them?"

"I cannot. The only reason I know Hans is guilty is because I saw him with a sock in his mouth yesterday."

"What did you do with your kids in all the rain?" asked Libba. I'm looking for ideas.

Daisy had more children than the woman who loved in the shoe. "Yesterday, we went to the mall and terrorized shop owners. I should have bought more socks."

"Is it clean socks or dirty socks?" I quickly organized my cards.

"It doesn't matter. He's an equal opportunity thief."

"And you can't find them?" That seemed impossible to me. Daisy had a large house, but between her brood of children and her husband, that was a lot of socks to go missing.

"I told the sitter I'd pay her double if she found them. Otherwise, I'll have to run to the Plaza and buy socks John can wear to work. The only pair he's got left are the ones on his feet."

I bit back a smile and counted my points. Thirteen with five hearts.

"One club." Libba opened the bidding.

"Pass," said Daisy.

"A heart," I replied.

Jinx eyed her cards. "Two diamonds."

Libba nodded. "Two hearts."

Daisy passed.

"Four hearts." I closed my hand and tapped the cards on the table's edge.

"Pass," said Jinx.

Libba passed, and Jinx played the ace of diamonds. "Who is the swim meet against tomorrow?"

"Belmont," Daisy replied.

"Do they still have a ton of swimmers?" she asked.

I nodded. "They do."

"Here or there?" Jinx took the trick and led the king of diamonds.

"There." Daisy and I spoke at the same time.

"Who is their swim chair?" Libba asked.

"Jill Turpin," I replied.

"I bet she runs an efficient meet."

The mean ones usually did. Something about being willing to scold or shame other women into efficiency.

Jinx led the queen.

"Ellison," said Daisy, "I heard Anarchy went into the Dixons' house when it was on fire."

I played the last diamond from the dummy and nodded. "He did."

Daisy played the six.

I trumped Jinx's queen with the two of hearts.

"You must have been terrified." Daisy's eyes were liquid and her frown empathetic.

"So scared I couldn't breathe. He rescued Percival. Which reminds me, do you know who Marian uses to take care of him when they're out of town?" I lead the three of hearts.

Jinx played a low heart. "No idea. You'd think the pet-sitter would have called and told her that the house is gone."

Exactly what I'd wondered. I played the jack of hearts from the board.

"Assuming she left a number," said Libba.

Daisy covered my jack with the queen, and I played the king from my hand.

"Has anyone seen Percival? Since the fire, I mean." Daisy caught her lip in her teeth. "I hate to think of him hungry and cold in the rain." That soft heart of hers was the reason she had a sock thief living in her house.

I played the ace of hearts from my hand, and Jinx tossed the last outstanding trump. After that, the remaining tricks were easy. "Made five."

Libba cut. Daisy dealt. Jinx shuffled.

"I heard that Leonard Dixon was having an affair." Libba

rested her elbows on the table and leaned forward. "Who do you suppose he was seeing?"

Jinx and I exchanged a loaded glance.

"Probably some woman from his office," said Daisy. "That or someone who got screwed in their divorce." She looked up from dealing and realized we were all staring at her. "What?" She sounded defensive. "He's not an attractive man. Either someone is in it for the money or someone wants to stick it to their ex-husband."

"Where did you lose your rose-colored glasses?" Jinx sounded impressed.

"They're with the socks. Missing." She studied her cards. "I'm just being pragmatic. One spade."

I needed five of a suit and opening count to overcall Daisy's bid. I didn't have either. "Pass."

"Four spades," said Jinx.

Libba closed her cards with a sharp rap on the table. "You two are playing spades. Ellison, who takes care of Max when you and Anarchy travel?"

"Aggie."

"Marian doesn't have a housekeeper?"

"She has a cleaning lady who comes every other Thursday."

"Is it possible she was supposed to take care of the cat?"

"That's a good thought. I'll see if Aggie knows who she is."

We played until three o'clock. When I arrived home, Aggie was gone, Grace was out (hopefully at swim practice), and Max wanted another outing.

"Have you behaved yourself?"

He wagged his tail.

"Fine. Let me change."

Five minutes later, we jogged down the drive. Both of us were willing to ignore the light mist in favor of exercise.

"I don't love running," I told him. "In the summer, I prefer to swim."

That was my problem, not his. He couldn't be bothered to care, and he pulled on the leash. Hard.

Finn and Beau Riley were a half-block ahead of us, and Max was determined to catch up.

I let him.

"Hi, Mrs. Jones." Like his dad, Beau wore a red wind-breaker, but his jacket did not have a crocodile.

"Hi, Beau. How are you?"

"My mom made me walk Finn." He flushed. "I mean, fine, thank you. How are you?"

"Grace is shirking her dog walking duties."

Max happily slowed his pace to walk next to Finn.

Where are you going?" I asked.

"The park."

"Me, too. Shall we go together?"

Beau nodded.

"How's your summer going?"

"The past few days were super boring."

I offered a sympathetic nod. "Too much rain."

"It makes everyone in a bad mood. My friend Brad's parents took him to a Holidome."

"That sounds like fun."

"Better than board games or cards. Mom said I should start my summer reading, but it's June."

"You don't read in June?"

"June is for the pool and tennis and golf. July is for camp. In August we drive to Colorado. I read on the way there and at the cabin. There's no TV."

I made a sympathetic noise as we stepped onto the path that surrounded the park. "Sounds like you have everything perfectly planned."

He shrugged. "I guess."

"Are you swimming at the meet tomorrow?"

"Yes." He glanced down at his feet. "Will you watch my

races?"

"Of course. What are you swimming?"

"Free, back, and medley."

"I'll be watching."

A small satisfied smile curled his lips. "Hopefully Mom comes. She missed the last meet because a friend from college came to town."

"If she's not there, I'll yell loud enough for two."

His grin lit his whole face.

Finn and Max walked happily together. Max didn't pull, and he ignored a squirrel only five feet to the right of the path.

The park smelled of damp earth, crushed rose petals, and pine. I breathed deep. "We should do this more often."

"I'd like that," said Beau. "Finn is easier when Max is around."

"And Max is easier when Finn is around."

We walked in companionable silence.

When we parted at the walk that led to his front door, I said, "I'll be there tomorrow. Cheering."

"You don't have to."

"I want to. Promise me, don't get embarrassed if I yell too loud."

His answering smile melted my heart.

CHAPTER TEN

The likelihood of my bidding and making a grand slam in bridge was small. The likelihood of me hitting a hole-in-one was even smaller. The chances of me beating the club tennis champion? Infinitesimal. The odds of all those things happening on the same day? A zillion to one.

And those odds were still better than getting nice weather for a swim meet.

Yet, here we were, gathered around Belmont's pool as the sun gently kissed our shoulders, a light breeze ruffled our hair, and the temperature hovered around seventy-five.

Jane Carson stood by my side. "Can you imagine if they were always like this?"

"Don't tease," I told her. "We need to savor this one perfect day." Because there would never be another, not for us. "Was it only last week that we melted?"

She nodded. "Later we watched the Dixons' house burn. Your husband is still investigating the fire?"

"He's investigating the death. Investigating the fire goes with that." I lowered my voice. "Did you ever hear the Dixons argue?"

"Heavens, yes."

"Often?"

"For years. Marian gets the same bee in her bonnet every spring. Leonard has been unfaithful."

"Has he?"

She shrugged. "Who knows? Every spring, he meets his college buddies for a golf trip. Hilton Head or Palm Springs or Palm Beach. And every spring, she accuses him of cheating."

"Every year?"

"Every year. Then he buys her some ridiculous owl figurine, and all is forgiven."

Did this change anything? I sipped my iced tea and watched the eight-and-under girls swim free. I still had a few minutes until Beau swam. "Have you seen Percival?"

"I have. Bill spotted him in the wreckage, and we lured him into our house."

"I'm so glad. I had nightmares about him being hungry and homeless. Did Marian have a pet-sitter?"

"For a while, when they traveled, Marian took him to board, but he was uninvited after an incident with a Siamese. After that, she asked me to check on him. Mostly making sure he had food in his bowl and water in his dish. If they were gone for more than a few days, I changed the litter box."

"She didn't ask you this time?"

"The balls, Ellison. I asked her to return the balls. We had words."

"Are those the ten-and-under boys?" A line of whip thin boys stood ready to mount the blocks.

"Who are you looking for?"

"Beau Riley. I promised I'd cheer for him."

"Poor kid. He needs someone cheering. Whit is a domineering ass."

"Repeating his own father's behavior."

"That makes so much sense." Her lips pursed. "What's Tippy's excuse?"

"What do you mean?"

"She forgot him at swim practice last week. Twice. I had to give him a ride home. Not that I minded."

It happened. Busy Schedules. Multiple demands. Mothers forgot. Once, when Grace was in grade school, I got involved in a painting and forgot to pick up a whole carpool. I couldn't throw stones at Tippy—not for that.

"Then Tippy asked me to give him a ride to the meet. She couldn't be bothered to bring him."

"I'm glad you were there. I'll tell Grace to keep an eye out too. She could easily give a ride to or from afternoon practice."

The boys climbed onto the blocks, and I called, "Go, Beau."

He grinned, offered me a tiny, slightly embarrassed wave, then put on his goggles.

The timer yelled, "Go!"

Beau dove into the pool and swam hard. His arms knifed through the water, and his legs kicked as if they'd never get another chance.

"You've got this!" I grasped Jane's arm. "He may win his heat!"

Beau was in the lead.

He executed a clean turn at the far end of the pool then maintained his speed.

I hopped up and down. "Go, Beau!"

His hand was the first to touch the wall. When he realized he'd won, he smiled as if he'd won Olympic gold.

The other swimmers finished the race, and Beau shook hands with the swimmers in the neighboring lanes before hauling himself out of the pool.

"Congratulations!" I trapped the boy in a hug, not caring about the sudden wet that soaked through my gingham shirt (red and white in the club's colors). "You were amazing!"

He freed himself and grinned at me. "Thank you for cheering. I heard you. It made me swim faster."

"That was all you, but I promise I'll be there for your next race."

He ducked his head, gave me a shy smile, and ran off with his friends.

"You don't get that excited when I win." Grace stood next to me, looking impossibly grown up in her red swim suit with a towel cinched around her waist.

"I'm always thrilled when you win." I was accustomed to Grace winning. So was she. For Beau, this win was a big deal. "But Beau needed this." Badly.

"Chill out, Mom. I was just teasing. It's really nice of you. Beau needs a cheering section." She was the second person to say that.

"I'll be cheering for you, too."

"I know, Mom. But it's okay if you cheer louder for Beau." She gave me a brief side-armed hug then disappeared into the crowd.

"She's a great kid," said Jane. "Speaking of which, I'd better check on my brood."

She left, and I adjusted my sunglasses and watched the next race.

"Ellison?"

I turned. "Jill." I'd hoped she'd be so busy running the meet that I could avoid seeing her.

"I'm glad I ran into you. It was such fun being with you and Anarchy at the Clarkes' dinner party. I had no idea your husband attended Stanford."

"Is that important?" My voice was as sweet as sugar.

Her smile matched my voice. "You understand."

I completely understood. People needed a reason to feel superior, and Jill had chosen education as her bar to entry.

"I remember high school. You could have gone to Wellesley like Tippy and me. Instead, you chose art school."

"Because I wanted to be an artist."

"That's what I wanted to ask you."

Was she seriously going to ask for a donation after insulting my education?

"I'm on the acquisitions committee for the school auction. Can we count on you for a donation this year?"

She hadn't bothered with a "please." Then again, what did I expect from Jill?

"The auction is in the fall?" I asked.

"Like always." Condescension made people want to do you favors. Not.

"I'll consider it." When pigs flew. Or when the heavens granted another perfect swim meet. A "maybe" was better than an outright "no."

She waved off my tepid reply. "You always give."

"That doesn't mean I'm obligated."

Her forehead creased as if she finally realized she might have a problem. "It's Grace's school."

"To which I write very large checks every semester."

"We all do that."

"I've donated a painting to the past ten auctions. Since Grace was in first grade."

"Which is why we're counting on you."

"I'm preparing for two gallery shows. I'll write a check instead."

Her eyes narrowed. "I told everyone I'd ask you."

"And you have."

"You've said 'yes' for years. To anyone who's come knocking."

I shrugged. "They said 'please.'" And they didn't denigrate my education.

"Please. Please, donate a painting. The auction for your pieces generates such excitement."

"I'll think about it." Nope. Not thinking. Not doing. "Now, if you'll excuse me, Grace has a race coming up."

Her hand snaked out and caught my arm. "Ellison."

"Grace has a race, Jill."

We stared at each other, and I saw rage swimming in her eyes. An anger so deep, it stole my breath.

She let me go, and I hurried away before she stopped me again.

I got up early on Thursday morning and swam. There was something soothing about watching the sunrise from the water. For me, it was better than meditation. I got bored after the tenth "ohm". I wished the pool deck was always so calm, even serene. Nothing like the controlled chaos of a swim meet.

My limbs cut through the rain-chilled water. My blood pumped. And when the sun broke the horizon, I tread water and breathed deep.

Feeling better than I had in a week, I returned home and parked in front of the house, knowing full well that Max waited at the door, expecting a run or at least a walk.

Except he didn't meet me.

"Max?" I called.

Aggie appeared in the hallway. "He's in the back yard."

I sniffed sugary air. "What's that smell?"

"I'm making French toast."

"French toast?" Grace and I were regularly donning swim suits. Neither one of us was indulging in French toast. And Aggie knew that. "Why?"

"Come look."

I followed Aggie into the kitchen. "What is it?"

"Look outside."

I glanced out the window.

Anarchy and Beau were playing catch. Beau wore a faded

tee-shirt and old gym shorts that I knew, without a shadow of a doubt, were not Tippy approved.

Finn and Max zoomed around the yard like lunatics, as if they had only ten minutes to get their lifetime fill of play.

"How did that happen?"

"He showed up here with Finn."

"And?"

Her expression clouded. "He mumbled something about his parents arguing."

"I see."

"He's too thin." Aggie crossed her arms, bunching her daffodil yellow kaftan. "Don't they feed him?" Now the French toast made sense.

"He's a ten-year-old boy. He can eat his weight in junk food and not gain an ounce." I'd seen him at the club snack bar. Frozen Snickers bars. Plates of fries drizzled with ketchup. Ice cream bars.

I poured myself a cup of coffee and pushed away the too enticing image of a frozen Snickers.

Beau's blond hair gleamed like spun gold in the morning sun, and Aggie watched him as if he were an angel come to earth. "What are his parents thinking?"

"What do you mean?"

"He's a beautiful boy, and he came to our house to escape them." Aggie opened the back door and called, "Can I interest anyone in French toast?"

"Me!" Beau called. Then he grinned at Anarchy. "Thanks for the pointers."

The two came inside, sat next to each other at the kitchen island, and drowned Aggie's perfectly cooked French toast in syrup.

Beau ate a bite and said, "Thank you, Aggie. This is the best breakfast I've ever had."

She flushed with pleasure. "I'm glad you like it."

"Do you make French toast every morning?"

"Nope. Your being here makes today a special occasion,"
Aggie told him.

"That's really nice of you to say." Beau didn't sound
convinced.

"She means it," I told him. "Aggie loves for people to appreciate her food, and Grace and I are always on some kind of diet."
Not strictly true, but it sounded good.

"I usually get cereal for breakfast."

I pretended not to see Aggie's wince. "What's your favorite
kind?"

"Cocoa Pebbles."

Anarchy lifted a glass of orange juice to his lip. "Because it
makes chocolate milk?"

"Yep." Beau took another large bite of French toast. When he
finished chewing, he asked, "What's your favorite cereal, Detective Jones?"

Anarchy looked over his shoulder as if he worried someone
might overhear. "Don't tell anyone, but I like Super Sugar
Crisp."

"What about you, Mrs. Jones? What do you like?"

I saved my sugars for cocktails and desserts. "When I eat
cereal, it's Cheerios."

He wrinkled his nose at my choice.

"I know. Boring. Occasionally I eat Grace's Corn Pops."

"Those are good. Dad likes Honeycomb."

I smiled at him. "What does your mom like?"

"She doesn't eat breakfast."

"Not everyone does," I replied.

"She takes these little pills then says she's not hungry."

The pressure women put on each other and themselves to be
thin and look pretty could be corrosive. It definitely wasn't
doing Beau any favors.

"So, if you don't eat cereal or French toast, what do you eat?"

he asked.

Coffee. "Fruit and maybe an egg."

"You eat that when Aggie will make you French toast?" He shook his head at my foolishness. "I bet she makes great waffles and pancakes, too."

"She does. And people would kill for her muffins."

His eyes grew huge. "Really?"

"No. I'm just teasing. No actual murder. But her muffins are delicious."

"The banana nut is my favorite," said Anarchy.

Beau ate his last bite, and Aggie immediately asked, "More?"

"Yes, please. I wish all our neighbors were as nice as you."

My heart warmed. "That's a lovely thing to say, Beau. Thank you."

"Who's not nice?" asked Anarchy.

Beau flushed.

"It's all right," Anarchy assured him. "I keep tons of secrets. Mrs. Jones does too. We won't repeat a word."

"Mrs. Dixon is mean. She and Mr. Dixon fight a bunch."

"You've heard them?"

"It's hard not to."

"Anyone else?"

"I think Mrs. Hamilton might be a witch," he whispered.

She was definitely a witch. A witch who was now in my corner. "If she is, she's the good kind." Sort of.

"Have you seen any of the neighbors going over to the Dixons' house?" asked Anarchy.

Beau frowned. "You mean since their house burned?"

"No. Before that."

"Mrs. Carson. She and Mrs. Dixon had a fight."

"About balls?" I prompted.

"No. Not balls. It was something else."

"Who else?"

"Mrs. Turpin. I was in the backyard one night and I saw her sneak through the Clarkes' gate."

"When was this?"

"Last week, I think."

"Which night?"

"After we got home from the swim meet, I was hanging my wet towel over the deck railing. That's when I saw her."

The night the Dixons' house burned. I glanced at Anarchy, but he wore a poker face.

"Mrs. Turpin is not very nice, either."

"No," I agreed. "She's not."

Beau ate another two slices of French toast then collected Finn. "I'd better get home."

"You are always welcome here," I told him. "You can come back anytime. Whenever you want."

"You're really nice, Mrs. Jones. Grace is super lucky to have you as a mom."

"And your parents are lucky to have you." Too bad they didn't act that way.

"Thank you."

When Beau left, I turned to Aggie. "What did Florence say?"

"She's never heard the Clarkes argue. Just the Dixons and the Rileys."

"The Rileys?"

"They live behind the Rhoades. And according to Florence, their marriage is on the rocks. No wonder that poor, sweet boy ended up over here."

There was so much to say about that, and none of it was good. I turned to Anarchy. "Jane Carson has Percival."

His brows lifted. "How?"

I took a moment and poured myself a fresh mug of coffee. "She and Bill saw him poking around the wreckage and rescued him."

"Pet-sitter?"

"She doesn't know. Jane took care of Percival until she and Marian had a falling out. Did you track down Virginia Minton?"

"Not yet."

"Hmm."

"What?"

"Plenty of people were mad at Marian, but we can't find anyone who wanted Grant dead." I stared out the window without actually seeing the backyard. "Didn't the aide say Virginia visited her mother on Thursdays?"

"She did."

"Then I guess I know where we'll be this afternoon."

CHAPTER ELEVEN

The clock on the dashboard read two o'clock when Anarchy parked his sedan in the lot at Pleasant Lane. He turned off the engine, but neither of us made a move to get out of the car. Instead, we listened to Melissa Manchester sing *Midnight Blue*.

The song faded, and I asked, "Do we have to tell Mary her son is dead?"

Anarchy groaned and rested the back of his head on his seat. "Not if we find Virginia."

"Then I hope she's here."

"You and me both."

The last time we'd visited Pleasant Lane, the building had smelled of antiseptic and urine. This time, the aroma of over-cooked vegetables joined the mix. I lowered my nose to the bouquet of fresh blooms I'd brought Mary. The flowers, each one selected for its scent, included lilies, stock (I adored the spicy clove-like aroma), and roses. Their combined perfume masked Pleasant Lane's unpleasant odor.

"Pardon me." I forced a smile.

The woman behind the front desk had blonde hair and dark

roots. She looked up from a crossword puzzle and frowned at me.

"We're here to see Mary Wycliff," I explained.

"Do you know how to get to her room?" She noticed Anarchy, took in broad shoulders and brown eyes, and her expression changed. "I'd be happy to show you."

I offered her a tight smile. "We know the way.

"Is Mrs. Minton with her?" Anarchy asked.

The woman sat straighter, amply demonstrating that her shirt was a size too small. "It's Thursday. She's always here on Thursdays."

"Thank you." He took a step back.

She fluttered her lashes. "You need to sign in."

"Of course." Anarchy picked up the pen and wrote *Mr. and Mrs. Jones*. Then he claimed my free hand, and we walked toward Mary's room.

We were halfway to Mary's room when I said, "I hate it when women do that."

"Do what?"

"Flirt with you."

Anarchy was nothing like my first husband. Nothing. I *knew* that. Watching women bat their lashes at him didn't make me jealous. Nope. I'd welcome jealousy. Instead, dread pooled in my stomach, and a dark part of my brain reminded me I'd failed to keep my last husband interested. Would Anarchy grow tired of me? Want someone prettier? Younger? My worry was not rational—intellectually, I was well aware my doubts were groundless—but emotions weren't rational.

As if he could sense my unease, Anarchy stopped us in the middle of the hallway. "I love you, Ellison. I always will. You're it for me. I wake up every morning and take a minute to watch you sleep."

"You watch me sleep?" Yikes. What if I drooled?

"I do. And I remind myself that I'm the luckiest man alive and I'd better not do anything to screw this up."

"That's...that's sweet. But I'm the lucky one."

"I could argue that with you all day." Gently, he pulled me out of the way of an older gentleman in a plaid bathrobe who barreled down the hall behind an aluminum walker. "Can we agree we're both lucky?" He tugged on my hand. "Come on, let's talk to Virginia so we can get out of here."

We walked past an open doorway that smelled worse than the hallway, and Anarchy's nose twitched.

"Do you want the flowers?" I offered him the bouquet.

His brows lifted in question.

"They help with the smell."

"Ah. You keep them."

We paused outside Mary's room and listened for voices. Hearing nothing, we tapped on the door and stepped inside.

"Ellison, how nice to see you." Mary sat in the Naugahyde recliner near the window. She wore a blue and white striped house coat. Her soft white hair looked freshly washed, and her eyes seemed brighter than the last time we visited. "Virginia, you remember Ellison Walford. She's dating Grant. He's taking her to prom."

Virginia Minton was a pretty woman with blonde hair, light brown eyes, and an apologetic smile. "Nice to meet you." She rose from the chair near her mother's and deposited a book on the seat.

"Likewise." I held out the flowers. "I brought these for you, Mary."

"They're beautiful, and they smell divine. We'll both enjoy them." Virginia took the bouquet and put it on her mother's bedside table then turned to Anarchy.

He held out his hand. "I'm Anarchy Jones."

The color drained from her cheeks.

"My husband," I said softly.

"You called me. You're with the police."

"You didn't call me back."

"You didn't say what you wanted."

I stared at her. If a police officer phoned me, I'd fall over myself in my hurry to return his call.

"I called about your brother."

"My brother?" A furrow creased her brow. "Why didn't you say so? What about Grant?"

"Is Grant here?" Mary looked around her oatmeal-colored room as if Grant were just out of sight. "Where is he? Why hasn't he come to see me?"

"I'm sure he'll come soon, Mom."

I was sure he wouldn't.

"Is there a place we could talk?" Anarchy asked Virginia.

Her gaze shifted to the window and its view of the lawn. A wrought-iron table surrounded by chairs sat under the shade of an old elm tree. "I hate to leave Mom."

"I'll stay with Mary," I offered.

Virginia gave a tiny resigned nod. "Mom, I'm going to talk with Ellison's husband for a few minutes. She'll sit with you until I get back."

Mary nodded, and Virginia and Anarchy left us.

I moved Virginia's copy of Alex Hailey's *The Moneychangers* to the bedside table and took the empty chair. "It's a beautiful day. We deserve it after so much rain."

"Is Grant still at baseball practice?"

Guilt pinched my stomach. If I told Mary that Grant was gone, would she remember tomorrow? Would a fresh wave of grief swamp her each time she learned of her son's death? I was not about to break her heart. "Probably."

She nodded, seemingly satisfied with my answer. "He's done well for himself, but I wish he didn't live so far away."

"Does he like Boston?"

"Doubtful. His wife is from there. She's too fancy to move to the Midwest."

"Olivia."

"That's right. Where's Harold?" She'd forgotten her husband's death? "Is he still at work? That man. Always working." She leaned forward. "That's why he doesn't like Virginia's fiancé. No work ethic." Mary narrowed her eyes. "The man makes furniture. That's a hobby, not a job."

They'd cut off Virginia because she married a carpenter? That was horrible. I hid my thoughts behind a polite smile.

"We gave her every advantage. Sent her to the best schools. Horses. Country clubs. Trips to Europe. And this is how she repays us."

The polite smile wavered. "Perhaps he makes her happy. Also, she seems like a devoted daughter."

Harold and Mary might have disapproved of Virginia's choice, but it was their daughter who'd moved back to the area, their daughter who showed up every week to visit her mother. Their golden boy came a few times a year.

"Girls—good girls—lose their minds in California. There must be something in the air. Girls who should date doctors or lawyers throw themselves at men who ride motorcycles and wear leather jackets." She leaned forward, and her hands clasped tightly in her lap. "They smoke marijuana. They wear clothes that leave nothing to the imagination. I told Harold we shouldn't let her go to USC." Mary's gaze landed on me. "You were never like that."

Mother would have snatched me bald-headed. "I was not like that." I'd followed all the rules.

"I was so pleased when Grant told me you'd agreed to go on a date with him—the prettiest girl in the class."

"Thank you for saying that." It wasn't remotely true.

"And so much more genteel than that awful Jill Tucker."

I'd forgotten that Grant took Jill on a few dates before he'd asked me out.

"That girl." Mary shook her head. "She has a mean streak a mile wide. I was relieved when Grant dumped her for you."

"I don't remember it that way."

"It's true. She called every night after he broke things off. For weeks and weeks. No pride." Mary sniffed. "Young ladies shouldn't call boys. I never let her talk to him. Not once. He'd moved on. He had you."

The rage I'd seen in Jill's eyes at the swim meet—had she been holding a grudge for almost twenty-five years? Did her anger include Grant? Beau had seen her headed to the Dixons' the night Grant died.

"What did she expect would happen after she disappeared into a closet with Whit Riley?"

"What?" My voice was too loud. "Whit and Jill? What about Tippy?"

"Tippy forgave Whit. Boys will be boys."

Boys will be boys. Nice boys could drink or sleep around or raise hell, and their mothers gave them a pass. Girls didn't get a pass. A girl who drank too much was a lush. If she slept around, she was a slut. If she raised hell, eyebrows lifted, and backs turned when she approached.

What a hypocrite Grant had been. He broke up with Jill for kissing Whit, then kissed my sister and expected me to forgive him. *Boys will be boys.* "Grant kissed Marjorie."

Mary shook her head as if she were preparing to impart bad news. She even patted my knee. "It wasn't Grant's fault. Your sister...has a zest for living. You should forgive him. He's a good boy."

Anarchy and Virginia's return saved me from replying. A good thing, since I doubted Mary would appreciate my calling her son a jackass. "Your mother was telling me your husband makes furniture."

Virginia, whose eyes were rimmed with red, searched my face before nodding. "Yes."

"Does he have a studio?"

"We bought a place in Raytown."

Mary huffed her displeasure.

"I'd love to see his work."

"Hold on." Virginia crossed to the bed, picked up a handbag, and fished out a business card.

"Thank you. Do I need an appointment?"

"It's best to call ahead."

"I'll do that."

"Ellison." Anarchy's hand pressed against the small of my back. "We should go."

"Mary, it's been interesting visiting with you." If I had my druthers, it would not happen again.

"You should give Grant another chance. He's a good boy."

"I'll think about it." Never. "Virginia, I'll call." I stepped closer to her and whispered, "I'm sorry for your loss."

"Thank you." For an instant, her eyes glistened, then she nodded, reclaimed her book, and took the empty seat next to her mother.

"Let's get out of here." Anarchy hurried me through the hallway and out into the sunshine.

As we walked to the car, I asked, "What did Virginia say?"

"You can tell Jinx to stop looking for the trustee. It was Grant Wycliff."

"Who takes over now that he's dead?" Because if it was his sister, she had a motive for murder.

"Virginia claims she doesn't know. Probably someone from the bank."

"Do you believe her?"

"I'm not sure."

"Wait." I held up a hand, halting our progress. "Grant was the trustee and refused to help his sister and her husband when they needed it?"

"According to Virginia, they've never had financial difficulties. Her husband's furniture is in high demand."

Had Whit lied about that? "What about Raytown?"

"They were able to buy a warehouse that he uses as a workshop and studio. They keep an apartment on the second floor. Virginia didn't need and doesn't want her parents' money."

"When did she last talk to Grant?"

"When they moved Mary to Pleasant Lane. If there was a problem with Mary's care or if there were bills that needed paying, Virginia communicated with Grant's secretary."

He glanced back at the nursing facility and hurried us to the car. "Let's get out of here."

When Anarchy pulled out of the parking lot, the tightness in my shoulders relaxed. "Mary and I had an interesting chat."

"Oh?"

"She reminded me that Jill and Grant dated in high school. He dumped her after she kissed Whit."

Anarchy's expression didn't change. He was unimpressed with my revelation. "Jill?"

"Tucker, then. Turpin, now. Beau saw her headed to the Dixons' last Wednesday."

"I'll talk to her, but I doubt something that happened twenty-five years ago is cause for murder."

I didn't argue the point. "When is Peters back from vacation?" Peters was Anarchy's grumpy partner.

"Why?"

"It can't be fun for you, interrogating our neighbors."

"He's back next Monday, but I don't think we can wait till then."

I stared out the window and, despite the beautiful June day, shivered. I had a terrible feeling Anarchy was right.

I rushed into the kitchen, tossed my handbag on the counter, and picked up the ringing phone. "Hello."

"Why are you out of breath?" Mother demanded.

"I ran for the phone."

"Where have you been?"

"Visiting Mary Wycliff at Pleasant Lane." I didn't add that Anarchy had gone with me. That would have required more explanation than I was willing to give.

Mother said nothing, and her silence spoke volumes.

"What?"

"New money, Ellison."

"I thought it came from oil wells."

"Yes," she admitted. "But the money is still new."

"You didn't say anything when I went out with Grant in high school." And Mother had had plenty to say about everything.

"You were sixteen. Hardly the age for a serious relationship."

"Tippy and Whit married."

"Don't argue with me, dear. I didn't say anything because the forbidden is always more attractive. Especially to teenage girls. If I'd told you that you couldn't see Grant, he would have been irresistible. Now, I called you because I learned, over the bridge table, that Grace won all her races yesterday."

"She did."

"And no one thought to call me?"

"Mother, if you care about her swimming, come to her meets."

"I do not appreciate hearing about my granddaughter's accomplishments from someone outside the family. It makes it look like we don't talk."

We talked plenty. Beyond plenty. "Grace won in free, back, breast and medley relay."

"Was that so hard?"

I rubbed the back of neck, trying—and failing—to release the gathering tension.

"Also," she continued, "what's happening across the street?"

"At the Dixons'?"

"Where else?"

"As far as I know, nothing is happening. No one has seen Marian or Leonard since before the fire."

"They can't expect you to live with that wreckage. It has to be some kind of safety hazard."

"Until the Dixons turn up, I'm not sure what I can do."

"If it were me, I'd be on the phone with the city." Of that, I had no doubt. "There must be a nuisance law."

"They lost their house and everything in it. I'm not filing a complaint after a week. Especially when they may not know it burned."

"What if they killed the man whose body was found?"

"Why would the Dixons kill Gr…" I stopped myself. "Why would the Dixons want the grief of dealing with a dead body?"

"What aren't you telling me?"

"I'm not discussing Anarchy's investigation."

"Be that way," she huffed. "How was your dinner at the Clarkes'?"

"Delicious."

"She had a private chef."

"Ethan Howe. He has two restaurants on the Plaza. And, as I said, dinner was delicious."

"I imagine they paid for it before things went to hell."

"Pardon?"

"Ward invested in some business deal that went south."

Poor Sally. "Did they…" Were they broke?

"They're fine. But there won't be any more private chefs or trips to Europe or new diamonds in Sally's ears in the foreseeable future."

Most people lived quite happily without those things. I

stretched the phone cord until I reached Mr. Coffee. His reservoir was full, and someone had filled him with grounds. I gave him a lover's pat then pushed his button.

"Ellison, are you there?"

"Yes."

"You didn't say anything."

"What do you want me to say? Sally is my friend, and I hate that this happened to her." It might explain why she got snockered at her dinner party.

"Has Sally said anything?"

"No." I crossed to the cupboard, selected a mug, then took the cream out of the fridge.

"What are you doing?"

"Making coffee."

"It's almost four o'clock."

"And?"

"Too late in the day for coffee."

"Speak for yourself," I snapped. Mother could bully me about many things, and I'd quietly take her abuse. But coffee was different. Special. Worth defending.

"Ellison!"

I swallowed a groan. "Mother, this conversation is not productive."

"Maybe if you didn't drink so much caffeine, you wouldn't be so prickly."

"Mother, I'm fairly certain that coffee is the only thing keeping me civil."

"Well!"

I said nothing.

"You obviously need a better attitude."

My attitude had been fine until this phone call.

Mr. Coffee wasn't finished perking, but I couldn't wait any longer. I poured a mug, added cream, took a sip, and gave a happy sigh.

"Back to Sally," Mother said.

"What about her?"

"Has she said anything to you?"

"You just told me. That was the first I've heard about it.".

"She's such a nice woman." Mother was fishing. For what? "Perhaps you should check on her."

"And say what? I heard Ward made a bad investment, and now you're short on dough?"

"There's no need to be vulgar."

"'Dough' is not vulgar."

"But it is slang."

I took another sip of coffee and considered trading it for a glass of wine. Or a bottle of gin.

Mother wanted something from me. That was clear. But what?

Asking would earn a sharp intake of breath, as if suggesting she had ulterior motives was offensive.

"I heard you declined a request for a painting."

News traveled fast.

"Jill Turpin pretty much demanded that I donate."

"It is for Grace's school."

"I'll write a check."

Her answering sigh tightened every muscle in my back. I abandoned the coffee mug on the counter. Wine or gin? Wine or gin? Did we have limes? What about tonic? I opened the refrigerator and found a bowl of cut limes covered with plastic wrap. Limes were great for gin and tonics, but I suspected they were cut with Grace's Tab colas in mind. "Aggie is the best."

"What does Aggie have to do with the school auction?"

"Nothing. Never mind. I said I'd think about a donation because Jill was rude."

"Don't shoot the messenger."

"I..." I bit my tongue. Much as I hated to admit it, Mother

had a point. If someone who wasn't Jill had asked me nicely for a painting, I'd have agreed. "I'll think about it."

"Is that the time? Your father is playing golf, then I am meeting them at the club for dinner." Her tone made it sound as if I'd delayed her by keeping her on the phone for too long.

"Have a lovely time."

"I expect to hear how next week's swim meet goes. "

"Or you could come and watch your granddaughter swim."

"Honestly, Ellison. Must you be so difficult? I will talk to you later." She hung up.

Wine or gin? Gin. Definitely gin. I grabbed the limes from the fridge then went in search of tonic and liquor.

CHAPTER TWELVE

Anarchy, Grace, and I had dinner together.

We sat in the breakfast room and devoured the hamburgers Anarchy had thrown on the grill and the salad Aggie had left for us. Grace had put frozen tater tats in the oven. I'd poured the drinks—beer for Anarchy, Tab with lime for Grace, gin for me (because, Mother).

"Thanks for getting Max out. Would you please do me another favor?"

"What?" Her tone was cautious.

"If you win any races at next week's meet, would you please call and tell your grandmother? One of her friends told her about this week's wins, and she'd rather hear about your successes from you."

She winced. "That's why the gin?"

I nodded.

"Sure, I'll call her." She dipped a tater tot in ketchup. "What did you do today?"

"Visited someone at Pleasant Lane."

"When I was little, our scout troop went on May day. We

took flowers to the residents." She wrinkled her nose. "That place smells funny."

I couldn't argue.

She turned to Anarchy. "What about you?"

Anarchy's burger hovered half-way between his plate and his mouth. "The investigation."

"Do you have any new leads?"

"We're working on it." He took an enormous bite.

"Do you know who died?" Grace persevered.

"Active investigation, Grace." He spoke around the food in his mouth.

That earned Anarchy an eye roll. Grace ate another tot then said, "I gave Beau Riley a ride home from practice this afternoon." For morning swim, practices were staggered by age group. In the afternoons, all the age groups were thrown together.

My lips flattened. "Tippy forgot him again? Someone needs to speak to her."

Grace and Anarchy stared at me. Expectantly.

"Me?" I reached for my gin and tonic. "I think Jane Carson would be better."

Grace gave a dismissive huff. "Mrs. Carson? I don't think so."

"Why not?"

"She might complain about Mrs. Riley, but she'd never confront her."

"She confronted Marian."

"That was different. Mrs. Dixon might be a busybody, but she's not terrifying. Not like Mrs. Riley. She's not going to put herself out for Beau."

"He's a great kid." Anarchy hit me with liquid, coffee-brown, please-call-Tippy eyes that melted my resolve faster than a chocolate bar left in the sun. "He needs someone to step up."

"You two should know that no mother appreciates having her parenting second guessed."

"That's just it," said Grace. "She's not parenting. And Beau's dad is—" Grace bit her lower lip and shook her head as if Whit were a personal disappointment "—his dad isn't nice to him."

I'd heard Whit harangue Beau at the swim meet, but was it worse than that?

"What do you mean, Grace?" Anarchy's gaze turned steely.

"Mr. Riley belittles him."

"Does he hurt him physically?" Anarchy looked ready to march over to the Rileys' house right this minute.

"Not that I know of, but words can hurt as much as fists. Sometimes more. Whoever came up with, 'sticks and stones may break my bones, but words will never hurt me,' was a complete idiot."

"Agreed," I murmured.

"So you'll talk to Mrs. Riley?"

"Yes."

"Tonight?"

"I'm sure dropping by unannounced to point out Tippy's parenting failures will not go over well."

"Then call her." Grace was not giving up.

"I think an in-person conversation might be best."

"I'm sure she's home. Call and invite her for coffee." The impatience of youth.

"Grace…"

"What? You're friends."

"Not friends. Friendly." Tipp and I shared history. We belonged to the same club. We lived in the same neighborhood. But we didn't seek each other out. We didn't call to talk or make plans for coffee or play bridge or golf or tennis together. We might chat at the grocer's or a cocktail party. We might stop on the sidewalk to say "hello." We might work together on a charity event or share a volunteer shift at the hospital. But if I had a problem, needed a shoulder to cry on, or wanted to share a triumph, I wouldn't call on Tippy.

Grace's bottom lip jutted. "This isn't something you can sit on. Beau needs you."

"I'll call her tomorrow. We'll make a date to meet in person."

"You can call her tonight." She got her stubbornness from Mother.

"Fine. I'll call her after dinner. Happy?"

She gave a grudging nod. "You like Beau. Don't you want to help him?"

"Of course I do." Mother would tell me that Beau lived in a beautiful home, had plenty to eat, and attended a private school. His parents were providing for him. And she'd be right. But Grace was also right. Whit was emotionally abusive. That meant Tippy should try harder. Instead she made a habit of forgetting her son. And I was the lucky woman who got to call her on it.

We finished our meal, and Grace said, "I'll clean up if you call Mrs. Riley."

"Fine." I left her and Anarchy with the dirty dishes and went to my desk where I kept my directories. The Rileys' phone number appeared in both the club and school books, but I took a moment before I dialed.

Tippy, it's Ellison. I'm calling to tell you that your parenting needs work.

That would not fly. At all.

Tippy, it's Ellison. Would you join me for coffee tomorrow morning?

And when she asked what prompted my invitation? What did I say then? After all, I'd never invited her for coffee before.

I leaned the back of my head against the desk chair and stared at the ceiling. When no easy answers appeared, I sighed, picked up the receiver, and called Tippy.

"Hello. Riley residence." Beau answered the phone.

"Hi, Beau. This is Mrs. Jones."

"Hi." I could hear the smile in his voice. "How's Max?"

"He's in the kitchen begging for leftovers from dinner."

"Finn does that, too. Mom says he's always underfoot."

"May I please speak with your mom?"

"Sure, I'll get her." Beau put down the phone.

A moment later, Tippy said "Hello, Ellison." If she was surprised to hear from me, I couldn't hear it her voice.

In my stomach, dinner churned. "Good evening. I was wondering if you might have time to join me for coffee tomorrow."

"What's the occasion?"

"There's something I'd like to discuss with you."

"That sounds ominous."

A nervous laugh escaped my suddenly dry lips. "Is ten o'clock okay?"

"Fine. Your house?"

"Aggie will bake."

"How can I refuse? See you in the morning."

"Looking forward to it." I was absolutely not looking forward to tomorrow's conversation. "If you bring Finn, the dogs can play."

We hung up.

"Well?" Grace stood in the entrance to the family room with her arms crossed over her chest.

"Tomorrow at ten."

Her posture relaxed. "Thanks, Mom. You're the best." More like a soft-hearted fool who was about to insult another woman's mothering.

Tippy arrived at precisely ten o'clock. She wore madras shorts, a pink polo shirt, and a guarded expression.

Max edged past me and welcomed Finn with a happy yip.

"Shall we put them out back?"

Tippy followed me through the house and watched as I put the dogs in the back yard.

"I set up coffee on the patio. I'll just grab this." I picked up a cake plate filled with muffins, and we stepped outside where the two dogs zoomed back and forth across the grass. The morning sun seemed gentle, and the scent of flowers wafted in the light breeze. I led Tippy to the wrought-iron table, and we took our chairs. "Cream or sugar?

"Black."

I poured her a cup of coffee then removed the glass dome from the cake plate. "Aggie made banana nut and lemon poppyseed."

Tippy selected a lemon poppyseed and put it on the plate already set at her place. "I shouldn't, but this looks too good to pass up."

"Worth every calorie." I poured my own coffee and helped myself to a muffin.

Tippy took a bite of her muffin and moaned. "Fabulous."

"I'm glad you like it." My nerves jittered as if I'd drunk too much coffee.

Tippy tilted her head to the morning sun. "Why am I here?"

This was the moment I'd dreaded since I'd called her last night. "Grace gave Beau a ride home from the pool yesterday."

"Please thank her for me." She picked up her coffee cup and sipped.

"Jane Carson mentioned she's done the same."

"What's this about, Ellison?"

"At our last home swim meet, Whit was harsh when talking to Beau."

Tippy put her cup on the table. "That's his way of motivating the boy. And it worked. Beau won two races at his last meet."

"Tippy, it was harsh. Even cruel. Do you remember how Whit's father spoke to him? How it hurt him?"

She nodded. Barely.

"This was worse."

"I can't change Whit."

"No." I leaned forward. "But you can be there for Beau."

"Pardon me? What are you suggesting?"

"Forgetting him. Repeatedly. He'll think you don't care about him."

Tippy pushed away from the table, and her chair's wrought-iron feet screeched across the bricks. "You invited me here to criticize my parenting?"

Exactly. "I invited you here because you have a great kid who needs you."

"You have no idea what I've been going through." She stood with her hands clenched at her sides. "Finn!"

Finn, who was rolling in the grass with Max, ignored her.

"Finn!"

The dog practiced selective hearing.

"Tippy—"

"No. How dare you?" She looked ready to rant.

"Because Beau's hurting."

That stopped her. Her fingers stretched then clenched. Stretched then clenched. Her chest heaved as if she'd just run a sprint. A deep flush traveled from neck to her cheeks. "I'm doing my best."

"Grace has committed to getting him to and from practice. What else can we do to help?"

She sat. Suddenly. Gracelessly. As if her knees had run out of strength "There are things…I can't…" She shook her head. "Thank you for offering him rides. That's kind of you."

"If things are tense at home, Beau is welcome here. Anytime. He can bring Finn."

"I couldn't ask you to do that."

"You didn't ask. I offered."

"Whit and I have—never mind. It doesn't matter."

"Just tell Beau you want Finn to burn off some energy playing with Max." I searched the yard for the two dogs. They both stared into the branches of an oak where a squirrel angrily scolded them.

"I never imagined my marriage could get so messy."

I resisted the urge to reach across the table. I doubted she'd appreciate the squeeze of my hand. "I understand messy. Henry and I were a catastrophe. He cheated, and I stayed. For Grace. I often wonder if she would have been better off if we'd divorced."

"Hindsight."

"Exactly."

She stood. "Finn!"

He ignored her.

"Let him stay. Beau can pick him up later."

"Thank you, Ellison. This couldn't have been an easy conversation for you." Her left hand hovered at her throat. "I'll do better. I will. Beau deserves my best." Her eyes glimmered. She turned her back on me and headed for the gate that led to the front yard. "I'll see myself out."

I collapsed in my chair. That had been stressful and emotionally exhausting and had gone better than I could have hoped. I took a bite of my muffin and groaned.

"Mrs. Jones." Aggie stood in the doorway to the kitchen. "You have a phone call."

I took another, much-needed sip of coffee. "Who's calling?"

"Kate Thomas."

"Ugh. Really?"

"You know what she wants?"

"I have a good idea." Kate was the school auction chairman.

I trudged into the kitchen with the cake plate. Leaving muffins outside when Max and Finn were on the loose was a terrible idea.

The receiver rested on the counter, and I picked it up slowly. "Hello."

"Ellison, it's Kate Thomas." I'd known Kate for most of my life. She was a year behind me in grade and high school. She was sweet and bubbly and a talker. "You can guess why I am calling."

I could. "Answer a question for me first."

"Shoot."

"Who put Jill Turpin in charge of acquisitions?"

"I guess I did. But I asked seven people, and they all said 'no.' Then she volunteered. What could I say? I take it she was her usual charming self?"

"Yep."

"Each year your donation is the highlight of the auction. Please, please consider supporting the school with a painting."

"It will be a small canvas." I didn't have the energy to say anything else.

"Thank you. So much. This means the world."

"My pleasure."

"We are so grateful. How's your summer going? Hey! You'll never guess who I saw last week."

"Burt Reynolds."

"I wish." She gave a long, lusty sigh. "Nope. I saw Grant Wycliff. Didn't the two of you date in high school?"

"We did. Where did you see him?"

"On our street." Kate lived one block over, on the same block as the Turpins and the Clarkes and the Rileys.

"When?"

"It was Tuesday. I remember because the next day his childhood home burned down."

"Was he with anyone?"

"No. He was alone. It was late afternoon, and he was just walking down the street by himself."

"Did you talk to him?"

"I called 'hello' but I don't think he heard me. He was on the opposite sidewalk, coming from farther up the block. Then he got in a rental car and drove away."

"What do mean 'up the block?'"

"Well, he walked down the block toward my house." Kate lived on the corner.

"He walked down the street and got in a car?"

"That's what I said."

"And drove away?"

"Yes. You sound odd. Is something wrong?"

"No. I'm fine." A complete falsehood. My gaze sought Aggie's and I pointed to Mr. Coffee. I needed a pick-me-up, a jolt to untangle the snarl in my brain. "You're sure it was Grant?"

"Positive."

I accepted a mug from Aggie and mouthed, "Thank you."

"Did you notice anything else?" I took a restorative sip.

"Like I said, I called his name, but he didn't hear me. He seemed very focused."

Grant Wyclif had met with someone. The day before he died. And he'd avoided parking in front of their house. Why? Who? And how could I find the answers to those questions?

CHAPTER THIRTEEN

I glanced out the window to the back yard where Max and Finn still played. Pansy, Max's girlfriend who lived with Charlie, had joined them. The three dogs looked deliriously happy as they trampled my annuals.

I considered scolding them. Instead, I picked up the phone and called Jinx.

We exchanged greetings, then she asked, "Anything new on the investigation?"

Nothing I could share without talking to Anarchy first. "Nope. But I learned something about the Wycliffs. Grant was the trustee."

"Interesting. Does that mean Virginia takes over now that he's dead?"

"Doubtful." I needed to call Virginia to see about visiting her husband's studio.

"Then who?"

"I assume a banker or lawyer. I have a question for you on a totally different subject."

"Okay. What is it?"

"Have you heard anything about the Clarkes' difficulties?"

She was silent so long I wondered if she meant to answer me. "Yes."

I wrapped the phone cord around my index finger. "Any idea what happened?"

"This is uncorroborated, but I heard Ward invested seven figures. The deal went bad."

"With whom did he invest?"

"Good question. I have a sense that it was with a firm on the east coast."

"Like Boston?"

"Could be. More likely New York. Why do you ask?"

Because Grant had pitched an investment to Whit. Because Grant and Ward had known each other since high school. Because I had a hunch. "No real reason. Have you heard of anyone else who was affected?"

"I think the Smarts."

"Julie and Robbie?"

"They didn't invest nearly as much as Ward."

Thank heaven for that. Fortunately, I knew just where to find Robbie. If I innocently ran into him, I could direct the conversation until he told me his investment advisor's name. And pigs flew. "Jinx, I promised the school auction a painting, which means I need to get to my studio."

"I heard Jill Turpin demanded a donation. I also heard you turned her down."

"Kate Thomas called."

"Of course she did." Jinx's chuckle was desert dry. "Let me guess, the auction simply won't be the auction unless you donate." She did a good Kate Thomas impersonation.

"Something like that."

"And you fell for it?"

"It's Grace's school."

"Right. I'll let you get to work."

We hung up, and I headed to my studio where I painted for a

few hours. As always, the application of color to canvas soothed me. When I went downstairs to change into golf clothes, I felt almost calm. Almost calm enough to ask Robbie, a man I considered a friend, leading questions.

Women were not allowed on the golf course on Friday afternoons, but we could use the putting clock and driving range. I chose the driving range. I knew Robbie would be there. Unless there was pouring rain or snow on the ground, the man teed off at two o'clock every Friday.

White balls waiting to be picked up dotted the range's grass. The sky was a cloudless blue. A light breeze kept the sun from being too hot. It was the perfect afternoon to be on the practice range. It would be even better if I were allowed on the course.

I let that little injustice go, took the spot next to Robbie, and put down my bucket of balls.

"Ellison." He nodded at me.

"Robbie." I flashed him a smile.

"Fun seeing you last weekend."

I nodded. "Delicious dinner."

"The lobster Pernod was excellent."

I took my three-wood from my bag. "Would you ever hire Chef Ethan for a private party?"

"A bit rich for my blood. I'll have to stick with his restaurants." He too had a three-wood, and he whacked his ball a country mile, as if the unsuspecting Titleist had somehow offended him.

"Sally and Ward were nice to treat us. I wonder if they'll hire him again."

Robbie attacked another ball. "Doubtful."

"Oh?"

"I don't know if you heard, but Ward had a financial setback."

"I hate to hear that." That was absolutely true. "What happened?"

"An old friend of his sold him on an investment that didn't work out."

"An old friend?"

"Grant Wycliff."

Drat. I hated being right.

Robbie looked at me funny.

"I knew Grant in high school. Even dated him for a while. I thought he lived in Boston."

"He does. When companies need capital to grow, sometimes they seek investors instead of loans. Grant helps match investors to companies."

"I see. So Ward invested in a company that failed?"

Whack! This time, when Robbie's wood connected, the ball soared.

I took a practice swing then hit my own ball which achieved only a third of Robbie's anger-fueled distance.

"Yes," said Robbie. "The company failed."

"And Ward has no recourse?"

"None." Bitterness laced his voice, and he hit another golf ball. Hard.

"That's too bad." I swallowed. "He can't sue?"

"Nope."

I swung my three-wood then watched the ball's trajectory.

"Nice," said Robbie.

"Nothing like your distance."

"I've got extra oomph lately."

Guilt held out a bony finger and poked me in the chest. But it was easier to gather a bit of gossip from Robbie than probe Sally and Ward's open wound. "Aggie is not Chef Ethan, but she's a fabulous cook. Would you and Julie join us for dinner sometime soon?"

Robbie's answering smile was warmer than the afternoon sun. "We'd love that."

"I'll call Julie, and we'll find a date."

Robbie glanced at his match. "I tee off in five." He slid his club into his bag. "Always a pleasure to see you, Ellison."

"Likewise."

He paused. "I shouldn't have shared Ward's business like that. I doubt he wants everyone in town to know his business."

"I won't spread it around."

"I appreciate that." He nodded and left.

I finished hitting the balls in my bucket then headed for home.

Not for one second did I think Sally and Ward had killed Grant. Nope. I refused to consider the possibility. Surely they weren't the only ones Grant had talked into investing. We just needed to find the others. I hurried inside to call Anarchy but stopped when I found Beau playing with two happy dogs on the Oriental in the front hallway.

The boy spotted me and paled. "I'm sorry, Mrs. Jones."

"For what?"

"Rough-housing."

"If it wears out Max, you can rough-house all you want."

He grinned. "Max never wears out."

"I'm well aware. But maybe you can achieve the impossible. He loves it when Finn visits. I hope you'll bring him more often."

"I don't want to be in the way."

"Never. We're glad to have you." I glanced at my watch. "What time is swim practice?"

"Four."

"I left something in my locker at the club. Would you like me to take you?"

He grinned. "That would be great."

"It's only three. You still have an hour before you swim, and Aggie made muffins this morning. Would you like one?"

He flushed. "I already ate two."

"Which did you like better, banana nut or lemon poppyseed?"

"Banana nut."

"Really? I'm a lemon poppyseed fan."

"Aggie said if I brought Finn tomorrow, she'd make cookies."

"Then you have to bring him. Aggie makes the best cookies ever. What's your favorite kind?"

"Peanut butter. What about you?"

"Chocolate chip."

"Those are good too."

"Sounds like a cookie date."

Max, who was not a licker, chose that moment to run his pink tongue from Beau's chin to his eyebrows.

"Ew, Max." Beau sat back on his heels, wiped his face, then wrapped his thin arms around Max's shoulders. "Thanks for the kiss, buddy."

My dog's tail wagged.

Finn nudged them both, and Beau included him in the hug.

Brnng, brnng.

Leaving the boy and the happy dogs, I hurried into Anarchy's study where I picked up the phone. "Jones Residence."

"It's me," said Libba. "I need a drink."

"It's three o'clock."

"Have you met Charlie's kids?"

"Not yet. Come at four-thirty."

"Why not now?"

"Three o'clock."

"You seem hung up on the time."

It was too early to drink. "I said I'd give Beau Riley a ride to swim practice."

"Why are you taking Tippy's kid to practice?

I glanced at the open doorway. "I left a pair of earrings in my locker, and I want to grab them. So I'm giving Beau a ride."

"That can't be true."

"Why not?"

"You're ridiculously careful with your jewelry."

"Leave it."

"Is someone listening?"

"Possibly."

"I want the whole story at four-thirty."

"Deal."

"I want a pitcher of martinis waiting."

"Done."

"See you then." She hung up.

When I emerged into the hallway, Beau had Finn on a leash.

"Are you leaving?"

He nodded.

"I'll pick you up at a quarter till four."

He frowned at the floor. "You're sure it's no trouble?"

I smiled as I lied. "None at all."

After I closed the door on Beau and Finn, I returned to the study, pulled the business card Virginia gave me from my handbag, and dialed.

"Minton's Fine Furniture. How may I help you?"

"Virginia? This Ellison Russell. I visited your mother—"

"Ellison. How nice to hear from you."

"I was wondering if I could come by tomorrow?"

"Absolutely. Would eleven o'clock suit you?

"Perfectly. I'll see you then."

We hung up, and I wondered if I might be wasting my time. I drummed my fingertips on Anarchy's desk and sighed. Virginia and Grant hadn't been close. She probably didn't know his business. But if she did...

~

Libba arrived at four twenty-five. "Where's the gin?"

"That bad?"

"You have no idea. They hate me."

"I thought you were crazy eights buddies."

"That was before I told them to put their dirty plates in the dishwasher." She planted her hands on her hips. "You're not my mother. You can't tell me what to do. You're just some woman. Dad will get tired of you soon."

I was so lucky. Grace and Anarchy had never had a problem. The two got along like peas and carrots. "Ouch. Living room or patio?"

"Patio." She frowned. "Where's Max?"

"Napping. Finn Riley was here most of the day, and Max is exhausted."

"Is that why you took Beau to practice? Quid pro quo for wearing out your dog?"

"Something like that." I led her through the kitchen, stopping along the way to pick up a tray of cheese and crackers and a pitcher of martinis.

"Is gin okay? I can make vodka."

"Like I'd be picky."

We settled at the wrought-iron table where I'd started my day.

Libba ignored the cheese and crackers, poured herself a to-the-rim martini, and sipped. "Ooh. That's good." Her shoulders loosened, and she gazed into her drink. "What if Charlie picks them?"

They were his kids. If Libba was horrible, he should pick them. But she wasn't horrible. Quite the opposite. "Give them time. They'll adjust."

"That's good advice." Sarcasm dripped from her voice, thick as honey.

My answering smile was sweet. "What else can I do for you?"

She exhaled, as if Charlie's kids had stolen her fight. "Be here. Be my friend."

"Always," I vowed.

"Take my mind off the whole mess. Tell me, has anyone located the Dixons?"

"Not yet."

"There's something you're not telling me."

"This stays between us."

"Cross my heart." She drew an invisible x over her chest.

"The body—it's Grant Wycliff."

"What? Explain."

"The body belongs to Grant. Last Tuesday, Kate Thomas saw him. He'd been visiting someone on her block."

"Whit?"

"If it was Whit, why did Grant park in front of Kate's house?" Kate lived on the corner. Whit lived in the middle of the block. "Also—never mind."

"You don't get to play that game with me. Spit it out."

"This cannot be repeated."

She drew another x.

"I mean it, Libba."

"Vault."

"Sally and Ward invested a lot of money with Grant, and he lost it."

"What's *a lot*?"

"Seven figures."

She whistled. "Do you think they killed him?"

"No." The word was out of my mouth before she finished her question.

The skin around her eyes crinkled. "Trying to convince me or yourself?"

"Also, Grant's sister is here."

"In Kansas City?"

"Raytown. Her husband makes furniture. I'm visiting his studio tomorrow."

"Wait." She held up an open palm. "A Wycliff married a carpenter?"

"A furniture maker."

"Potato. Potahto." She lowered her sunglasses, peered at me over the rims, and grinned. "That must have driven Mary bonkers. In high school, she was so pleased that Grant dated you. Someone from the old guard." A la-di-da accent highlighted Libba's opinion of Mrs. Wycliff.

"She did not say that."

Her grin widened. "She totally did. Did the sister have a reason to kill Grant?"

"Harold cut her off when she got married." I ignored Libba's *well-duh* snort. "After Harold died, Grant became the trustee of Harold's estate. He didn't give her a dime."

"Sounds like she had a motive."

"Maybe. But why was Grant's body in the Dixons' house?"

"It used to be the Wycliffs' house. Maybe the sister was sending some kind of message."

"Her name is Virginia, and I like her."

Libba reached forward and patted my hand. "It wouldn't be the first time you've liked a killer."

Unfortunately, she was right.

I took a sip of my martini, noticed that Libba's drink was almost empty, and refilled her glass.

"What are we drinking?" Anarchy joined us on the patio.

"Martinis. Want one?"

He held up a long neck bottle. If Mother were here, she'd suggest I fetch him a glass—the suggestion a not-subtle criticism for both of us. Anarchy for drinking beer from a bottle. Me for letting him.

He pulled out a chair. "How did it go this morning?"

"Better than I expected."

He reached for my hand and squeezed. He might want the details of my conversation with Tippy, but I had other things on my mind.

"Kate Thomas called me this morning."

"Who?"

"Kate Thomas. She lives on the corner." I pointed to my left. "Next block over. She saw Grant last Tuesday."

Anarchy sat straighter. "She called to tell you that?"

"She called to secure a donation for the school auction. She mentioned Grant because we dated in high school."

Anarchy mumbled something about Peyton Place.

"The interesting thing is that he parked in front of Kate's house but came walking down the street."

"So?" Libba frowned at me.

"He didn't park in front of the house belonging to the person with whom he met."

"With whom he met?" She shook her head. "You've been spending too much time with Frances."

I ignored her dig. "The point is, Grant was being shady. Then the next day, he died."

"So, who did he meet? Whit?"

"Why would he hide meeting with Whit?"

"Who else? Oh." She went so far as to put down her glass and cover her lips with her palms. "Sally and Ward?"

"The Clarkes?" Anarchy frowned in confusion.

"They invested a significant amount of money with Grant," I replied. "Which he lost."

Libba reclaimed her glass and took a large sip of her martini.

Anarchy's frown deepened. "When did—"

"Today. I tried calling, but they said you were out."

"I met with the banker who'll take over as the trustee now that Grant is dead."

"And?"

"Upon Mary's death, Grant's children would inherit."

"Virginia was disinherited?"

"So nouveau," said Libba.

Anarchy stared at her.

"New money is desperate to distance itself from anything too close to its roots."

"The Wycliffs' money came from oil," he replied. "Not wood-working."

"Harold Wycliff's father was a wildcatter, but his son attended Harvard and married a Brahmin. They'd made it. No lowly carpenters for them."

"It does mean Virginia lacks motive." That was good news.

Anarchy reached for my hand. "I'm afraid that leaves your friends the Clarkes as our only persons of interest."

That called for another sip of martini. A large one.

CHAPTER FOURTEEN

I moaned. Long and low and pitifully. Then I burrowed deeper into my pillow.

"That's what you get for drinking with Libba."

"You're my husband. Aren't you supposed to be sympathetic?" True, I'd done this to myself, but I needed sympathy.

"I brought you coffee."

I slitted my eyes, determined that Anarchy actually held a coffee cup in his hands, pushed myself to sitting, and made a *gimme* motion with my hands.

"Hold out your palm," he instructed.

I did as he requested, and he shook two drugstore painkillers onto my hand.

I tossed them back then claimed the coffee and washed them down. "Thank you, thank you, thank you." Last night had been a mistake. An epic mistake. Lesson learned. Also learned? Coffee was better than sympathy. "What happened to Libba?"

"She's asleep in the blue room. I couldn't let her drive, and she refused to go to Charlie's."

"She's having problems with his kids."

His eyes twinkled. "She might have said something about

that. I told her she should bribe them with Aggie's cookies."
That was genius. Much better than my advice.

I took another sip of the nectar of the gods (coffee might not
confer immortality to mere mortals, but it did offer clarity).
"They're only here for a few weeks." It was a good thing Aggie
enjoyed baking. "Then they go to camp. Someplace in Colorado,
I think."

He frowned as if he'd never before considered camp. "Grace
doesn't go to camp."

"Not anymore. She went to a camp in Minnesota for seven
or eight summers. The same place I went as a girl. They have it
all—sailing, horseback riding, archery, trap shooting, kayaking,
arts and crafts."

"Sounds great. What happened? Why did she stop going?"

"She said she didn't want to go."

He tilted his head as if he didn't understand my answer.
"Why?"

I stared into my mug. "Things were rough between Henry
and me. I think she wanted to stay home to make sure I was
okay." I'd argued with her. Begged her to go. But she stood firm
in her decision. "Children shouldn't have to worry about their
parents. I hate that she missed out because of me."

"Ellison, Grace is happy, well-adjusted, and an all-around
great kid. Let it go."

"You're right. You're right. But—"

"No, buts. Now, finish your coffee. Are you hungry? Aggie
spent the night at Mac's, but I can manage bacon and eggs."

"She's coming back, right? She promised Beau cookies, and
peanut butter are his favorite."

"Not oatmeal?" Disappointment dragged down the corners
of his mouth. Anarchy liked oatmeal cookies. With raisins. It
was one of his few flaws.

"Peanut butter."

"That's a shame, but I guess I'll make do."

"What's your plan for the day?" I hoped he didn't have to work.

"What are you doing?"

"Visiting Virginia Minton's husband's studio."

His brown eyes widened. "By yourself?"

"You could come with me."

"What time?"

"Eleven."

"It's nine now."

I gasped. "It can't be!" I turned to look at the clock and regretted the sudden movement when my head threatened to explode. I clutched my free hand to my skull.

"What's wrong?"

"Headache."

"Drink some water." He nodded to the full glass on the bedside table.

I tightened my grip on my mug as if I feared he'd try to take it from me.

He chuckled. "Keep your coffee. I'll fix breakfast while you take a shower and get dressed." Anarchy was already showered. He smelled of soap and clean linen and wore khaki pants and a polo shirt I'd bought him at Jack Henry's.

"So you're coming with me?"

"Wouldn't miss it."

"I got lucky the day I met you."

"You found your first body the day you met me."

I grinned at him. "Doesn't mean I wasn't lucky."

He leaned forward and kissed me. "Go shower."

"Fine," I grumped.

Showering felt good. Brushing my teeth felt better. And by the time I descended the stairs to the kitchen, the aceta-minophen had kicked in, and I felt almost human.

A plate of bacon and eggs waited for me on the island next to yesterday's muffins. I selected a lemon poppyseed.

"Here you go." Anarchy put a fresh cup of coffee next to my plate. His preference for raisin-studded oatmeal cookies aside, I really had found the perfect man.

"Thank you."

Max, obviously rejuvenated from his nap followed by a good night's sleep, watched me lift the bacon to my lips. How could I eat something so delicious without sharing?

Because I had a hangover. I heartlessly ate the whole strip. When I finished breakfast, Anarchy took my plate, rinsed it, and put it in the dishwasher. "Feeling better?"

"Much."

"You know you're a lightweight?"

"I am aware."

"You know Libba is not?"

"I'm well aware."

"You had two drinks, Ellison. Two. She had—"

"What's your point, Detective Jones?"

"So it's detective now?" He grinned.

I crossed my arms and attempted to look tough. "Answer the question."

"No point. Just making an observation." He grabbed Mr. Coffee's pot and refilled my mug. Perfect man.

"I should stick to wine. Or coffee."

"Exactly. Martinis are not your friend." He glanced at the kitchen clock. "How long will it take us to get to Raytown?"

"I'm not sure. I need a city map."

"What? You know where everything is."

The benefit of being born and bred. "Not in Raytown, I don't. We drive east on 63rd Street. Beyond that, I'm lost."

Anarchy located Virginia's husband's studio on a map, studied the route, and asked, "Ready to go?"

"You know how to get there?"

"I can find it."

"Raytown's tricky."

"Why?"

Because it wasn't Kansas City. "It just is."

"I can find the way."

"Then let's go."

The drive took nearly thirty minutes. And if we drove by the same gas station twice, I was smart enough to keep my mouth closed.

Minton's Fine Furniture was housed in a small warehouse.

Anarchy knocked on the metal door, and Virginia opened it. Her expression flickered when she saw my police detective husband, but she quickly manufactured a smile. "Please, come in."

We stepped into a well-lit showroom filled with stunningly beautiful furniture. A desk called to me. Who was I to resist its invitation? I circled it, studied its elegant lines, then ran my fingers across its satin surface. "This is beautiful."

"Thank you." The voice didn't belong to Virginia.

I turned and saw an enormous man with an auburn beard and bright blue eyes. He wore a scarred leather apron over a worn pair of jeans and a denim work shirt. "I'm Aaron."

"Nice to me you. I'm Ellison Jones." I held out my hand.

His hand—his catcher's mitt—swallowed mine. "Welcome to my studio."

"Your work is beautiful." Aaron wasn't a carpenter. Nor was he a furniture maker. He was an artist. "Is the desk for sale?"

"To a good home."

"Mine is a good home."

"Fifteen hundred."

"Sold!"

"You're supposed to haggle."

I waved that ridiculous notion aside. "I'm too in love."

He grinned. "Virginia said I'd like you. She said you're an artist."

"Ellison's a painter." Anarchy sounded proud. Of me. Mother

considered my art to be a hobby that had gotten out of control. Grace treated it with the casual indifference of a teenager who'd grown up with her mother daubing at canvas. Henry had approached my painting and success with sneering disdain. Pride was new.

"Are you?" Aaron wore a guarded expression, as if he worried I'd whip out a stack of sketchbooks so he could admire my work.

"She's famous, Aaron." His wife's voice was gentle. "She paints under the name Ellison Russell."

"Oh. Wow. I know your work. You're good."

"Better than good." Anarchy's fingers brushed our new desk —his new desk. There was no reason he should use Henry's old desk (which was the size of a warship and ugly to boot). "You made this by hand?"

"I did. Would you like to see my workshop?"

Anarchy nodded. "I'd like that."

"Ellison, coffee or workshop?" asked Virginia.

"I never say no to coffee." I'd ask for the workshop tour the next time I came.

"This way." She led me to a small kitchenette and took two mugs from a cabinet.

"Your husband is charming and incredibly talented."

She blushed a pretty shade of pink. "He is. We've been very happy."

"Happiness makes up for a lot."

Her expression turned sad, as if she were thinking of broken relationships—her father, who'd cut her off, her dead brother, and her mother who seemed lost in her own mind. She gave a brief nod. "It does."

"My first husband and I weren't happy. Being with Anarchy is a second chance."

"Your first husband was Henry Russell?"

"Yes."

Her lips thinned. "I knew of him. I'm glad you're happy now."

I liked this woman. A lot. She reminded me of Libba. Not on the surface (Libba would never wear the slightly Bohemian dress that hung from Virginia's shoulders), but where it counted. I felt as if I could trust Virginia Minton. She was solid. To the core. I was sure of it. "I should tell you, Anarchy found the other trustee."

"Thank heavens. I've been worried about my mother's care."

"I know the terms of the trust."

She shrugged. "Let me guess. I get nothing. I made my peace with that years ago. I didn't expect my father would leave me more than a nasty letter."

"But you take care of your mother."

"Someone has to."

"I am sorry."

"Don't be. I'm the lucky one. I have Aaron. We're happy. And we have a marvelous life together. I'd rather have that than wealth. I saw Grant from time to time. He was rich, and he was miserable—married to a woman he didn't love, stuck doing a job he didn't like."

Lots of men got caught in jobs they hated. They married, bought a house, and had children. Then, when obligations weighed them down, they discovered that being an accountant or lawyer or doctor wasn't for them. But it was too late. They had mortgages and tuitions to pay. Teeth to straighten and country club due at the end of the month. They were stuck. But marrying a woman he didn't love? "Why did Grant marry her?

"I saw him a few months before he asked Olivia to marry him. The girl of his dreams had broken his heart, and he told me he didn't much care who he married if he couldn't have her. Olivia was guaranteed to please my father. Old Boston. Educated at Vassar. And her father owned a successful private equity firm."

"Did Olivia love him?"

"I honestly don't know. Aaron and I weren't invited to the wedding. There was no way my parents wanted a man who worked with his hands rubbing elbows with Boston's elite." She winced then shook off the expression and poured coffee. "I sound bitter. I'm not. But I did miss my little brother, and I wish he'd found happiness."

I nodded and sipped from the mug she handed me. "Wow. This is wonderful coffee." So much easier to talk about coffee than her horrible parents and the ways they'd wounded her.

"Thank you. Aaron loves his coffee. He found an importer who gets him special beans."

I adored these people. Virginia was smart and articulate. Aaron was an artist who loved coffee. "I know it's terribly short notice, but would you and Aaron like to join us for dinner? My housekeeper is a marvelous cook, and Anarchy grills a mean steak."

"You don't cook?"

"My family has banned me from even attempting it."

"Tell me how you managed that."

I'd charred pot roasts. I'd turned out scrambled eggs so tough that Henry had chipped a tooth. I'd filled the kitchen with smoke so many times that we had to repaint the ceiling and walls. "A few mishaps."

"I've had a few mishaps, but Aaron and I still split the cooking."

"Set a kitchen on fire."

She grinned.

I didn't.

Her grin faltered. "You're not kidding."

"I am not."

"You're sure we wouldn't be putting you out? For dinner, I mean."

"We'd love to have you."

"In that case, yes. Aaron can put the desk in the back of the truck, and we'll bring it to you tonight. What time?"

"Six?" I suggested.

"Looking forward to it already."

I sat at the wrought-iron table on the patio, sipped fresh lemonade, and watched Beau throw balls for Finn and Max.

On his own, Max did not play fetch. He adopted an if-you-want-it-why-did-you-throw-it, get-it-yourself attitude and refused to retrieve. But with Finn and Beau, he chased balls with the enthusiasm of a two-year-old Labrador.

I stood, adjusted the tilt of the sun umbrella, and sank back into my chair.

Finn bypassed Beau, ran to me, and dropped a slobbery tennis ball in my lap.

"Yuck." I hurled it as far as I could, and Finn took off running.

"Did he mess up your dress?" Beau's face twisted with worry.

"Not in the slightest." I wore a cool cotton print. "It'll dry. Now, if I had on a ball gown, I might not be as blasé."

"Mom hates it when Finn gets her dirty."

"Really, Beau. I don't mind."

Relief relaxed his features.

"More lemonade? Your friends are taking break." The dogs had collapsed in the shade. They panted heavily, and their pink tongues called from their grinning mouths.

"Yes, please."

I refilled his glass, and he reached for another cookie.

"Nope. You want a cookie, go wash your hands." He'd been tossing a ball covered with dog slobber for at least half an hour.

"Be right back." He made a run for the house.

Grace stepped outside as he disappeared into the kitchen.

She took in the exhausted dogs and said, "He wore out Max? Again?"

"He did."

"We should keep him."

"His parents might object."

"*Pish*. I always wanted a brother."

"That ship has sailed. What are you doing tonight?"

"Babysitting for the Oakes."

"Are you home for dinner?"

"Nope."

Beau emerged with freshly washed hands. "May I have a cookie now? Please?"

"Of course."

Anarchy stepped outside and gave a small worried shake of his head. Five-thirty and the Rileys still weren't home.

I'd hoped my chat with Tippy would have her upping her parenting game. Instead, she appeared to have given Beau to me.

He'd been with us since one, and he'd stay with us until someone came home.

"Beau, Anarchy bought too much steak. Especially since Grace won't be home for dinner. Would you stay and help us eat it."

"I couldn't."

"You could. He's also grilling corn on the cob. Aggie made potato salad, cornbread, and strawberry shortcake for dessert."

His eyes rounded. "Strawberry shortcake. With whipped cream?"

"Yes."

"Mrs. Jones." Aggie stood in the doorway to the kitchen. "Telephone call for you."

I stood. "Think about it, Beau. I'll be back in a minute."

I stepped inside and picked up the phone. "Hello."

"Ellison, it's Jill Turpin."

Drat.

"I may have been brusque when I approached you for a donation for the auction. I'm calling to apologize."

That had to eat at her.

"Thank you for donating a painting."

"My pleasure." Sort of. I'd been guilted into it. "Jill, while I've got you on the phone, may I ask you a question?"

"Go ahead."

"Have you seen Grant Wycliff lately?"

"No!" Too strong. Too loud. "Why would you ask that?"

"You're sure you haven't seen him?"

"I told you I hadn't." Jill's temper was showing.

I'd only asked because I'd wondered if, like Kate, she'd seen Grant walking down her block. Her vehement response posed new questions. "Wonderful. I'll let Anarchy know."

"Anarchy?"

"Grant was on your block last week."

"So?"

"We'd like to talk to him about the fire."

"Why would Grant burn the Dixons' house?"

He hadn't. I made a small, maybe-this-maybe-that noise.

"Whoever says they saw him is mistaken," Jill insisted.

"You sound very sure about that." Too sure.

"Everyone makes mistakes, Ellison."

"Anarchy will be in touch."

She hung up.

I stared at the dead receiver. What was Jill hiding? A bad investment? An affair? I hung up the phone and returned to the patio where Anarchy and Beau sat at the table and the dogs lounged on the shaded bricks.

"Who called?" asked Anarchy.

I reclaimed my seat. "Jill Turpin."

His brows rose in question.

"I'll tell you later. Beau, you told me you go to camp. Where do you go?"

"It's in Minnesota."

"What's your favorite activity?" I asked.

"Sailing and archery."

Memories of skimming across a cold Minnesota lake sparkled like sunshine on the water. "I used to love sailing."

"Me, too," said Anarchy.

I stared at my husband. "I didn't know you sailed."

"I'm from California."

"I suspect there are plenty of people who live in California who don't sail."

Anarchy and Beau exchanged what-a-ridiculous-statement grins, and Anarchy said, "Doubtful."

"Maybe we can head down to the Lake of the Ozarks or Table Rock Lake and rent a boat."

"Won't be the same as sailing on the Pacific."

"Well, those lakes are only a few hours away. The Pacific would take more doing." Plus, his family was in California, and I liked keeping half a country between us.

Anarchy smirked as if he'd read my mind. "You ever been to California, Beau?"

"No."

"I'm from northern California, near San Francisco."

"Is it always sunny?"

"Nope. That's Los Angeles and San Diego. San Francisco gets plenty of fog."

"Why'd you come to Kansas City?" asked Beau.

"I was looking for something."

"Did you find it?"

Anarchy smiled at me. "I did."

"Mrs. Jones." Aggie stood at the kitchen door again. "Your guests are here, and they brought a desk."

Anarchy and I stood.

"Should I go home?"

I rested my hand on Beau's shoulder and squeezed. "I'm not sending you home to an empty house. Besides, you promised to stay for dinner."

Anarchy and I walked inside and met Virginia and Aaron in the front hall.

After the usual flurry of hugs and kisses, Virginia said, "The house." She'd grown up across the street.

"You hadn't seen it? I'm sorry."

Tears shimmered in her eyes, and she wiped them away with a quick dash of her hands. "I knew I couldn't go home again. I'm being silly."

"No, not at all. It was your childhood home. Would you care for a drink?"

"Yes, please."

"It's so nice outside, we've set up on the patio."

"Anarchy," said Aaron, "want to help me move a desk?"

"Sure thing. We'll join you on the patio in a few minutes."

Virginia and I stepped outside, and she froze.

"Virginia, are you okay?"

"I'm sorry. Is that your son?"

"Beau? He belongs to a neighbor, but we adore him. He brings the Airedale, Finn, to play with our Weimaraner, Max."

She stared at the boy playing tug-a-war with a rope and two dogs and nodded. "The dogs wear each other out?"

"Exactly."

"Beau." Anarchy stepped onto the patio.

Beau released his grip on the rope.

"Your mom called. She wants you home."

The boy's face fell.

I wanted him to stay, but getting into an argument with Tippy when we had guests wasn't the best plan. "Come over tomorrow. We'll save you some strawberry shortcake."

"Really?"

"Promise."

He grinned and attached a leash to Finn's collar.

When he was gone, Virginia sighed. "Cute kid. We grew up with Airedales."

"I remember. Oswald."

She laughed softly. "That's right. Seeing him reminded me."

"What can I get you to drink?"

"Can you make a gin martini?"

CHAPTER FIFTEEN

I poured my second cup of coffee and glanced at the clock. Anarchy had been gone longer than I expected.

Did you have fun last night?

I smiled at Mr. Coffee. "We did. The Mintons are a lovely couple."

He's a coffee drinker like you?

"He is."

Good man.

Anarchy entered the kitchen and raked his fingers through his hair. "That woman."

"I did warn you."

"I've met nicer convicts." He held up a hand. "I know. I know. You warned me."

"Did she admit to seeing Grant?"

Anarchy had started his Sunday morning with a visit to the Turpins. "She did."

"So why did she lie to me?"

"She claims Grant threatened her."

The Grant I knew was a lover, not a fighter. "With what? Revealing a secret? Burning her house? Murder?"

"She refused to tell me."

"Do you think she killed him?"

He poured himself a cup of coffee. "Not sure."

I tightened the tie on my robe. "I think she did it."

Anarchy's lips quirked. "Is it possible your dislike for Jill is influencing your opinion?"

"What do you mean?" I knew exactly what he meant.

"As far as we know, she has no motive."

"Grant threatened her, and she had opportunity."

"Everyone on the block had opportunity. It was the middle of the night. Anyone could have dragged Grant to the Dixons' house, broken in, then set the place on fire."

"Wait. You're saying one of our neighbors killed Grant?"

Ding, dong.

It was Sunday morning. I glanced at the clock. Barely ten. "Who comes to the door on Sunday morning?"

Anarchy grinned. "I did."

"Yes, but you're a detective."

"Maybe it's Peters."

Ugh. I hoped not. I needed a few more cups before I dealt with Anarchy's partner's air of disapproval.

Ding, dong.

Max lifted his head from his paws, yawned, and gave us an are-you-going-to-answer-that look.

I pushed away from the island and strode into the front hall. "Oh dear Lord."

"What?" Anarchy was right behind me. "What's wrong?"

"It's Marian Dixon." I could see her through the glass panels that flanked the front door. "Can we pretend we're not home."

"She's seen us."

I sighed as my hand clasped the handle, then I turned the knob.

"What happened?" Marian screeched like one of the owls she so loved. "Where's Percival?"

"Jane is taking care of him."

"Thank heavens." She leveled a death glare at the center of my face. "What happened to my house?"

"There was a fire."

"I can see that, Ellison. When?"

"The night you left."

"No one called us?"

"We didn't know where you were."

Max ambled into the front hall. He and Marian weren't friends, and his appearance did not improve her mood. Her face turned as red as the bricks that led to my front door.

"Do you know a man named Grant Wycliff?" Anarchy asked.

"We bought the house from the Wycliffs." She frowned. "Grant? Is that the son? Don't know him."

"No idea why he'd be in your house?"

She pressed her palms to her ample bosom. "Did he start the fire?"

"No."

She shifted her death glare to Anarchy. "Then why are you asking?"

"His body was found in your home."

For a few seconds, time stopped, then Marian turned and bellowed, "Leonard!"

Leonard Dixon, who stood in his front yard with his head bent and his hands jammed in his pockets, didn't respond.

"Leonard!" Louder still.

He definitely heard her. People across the state line heard her. He chose to ignore her.

"Leonard Dixon!"

The windows rattled.

"Someone died in our house."

He turned and stared at his wife. Then, slowly, deliberately, he walked to the car he'd parked at the curb and opened the driver's side door.

"Leonard!"

He slid behind the wheel.

"Leonard!"

He drove away.

We all stared at the spot where Leonard had parked. As if he might come back. As if we'd imagined him leaving his wife.

Marian turned to me and pointed a fleshy finger at my chest. "This is your fault."

"My fault?"

"For a whole year, nothing but death and drama. Who finds bodies every week? No one. No one. But. You." Her finger met my sternum. Hard enough to leave a bruise.

"Unless you want to be arrested for assault, keep your hands off my wife."

Marian blinked then sneered. "You're going to arrest me?"

"It would be my pleasure." Anarchy's tone was as cold as a grave.

Marian took a step back and planted her hands on her hips. "It's her fault. I've watched her. She acts like a regular woman, but she's a magnet for murder."

"Mrs. Dixon, you have ten seconds to get off our property." Anarchy's voice was terrifying. If I were Marian, I'd run.

She retreated only a few steps.

"Last warning."

Marian turned on her heel just in time to see Mother park her Mercedes at the curb. Her sturdy legs carried her toward my mother's car at a breakneck pace. When Mother emerged, she said, "Frances, I me so glad you're here. Your son-in-law threatened me."

Mother stared at her. "Why?"

Marian made a choking sound, and I wished I could see her

face. Chances were good her mouth was opening and closing like a goldfish.

Mother's eyes narrowed and her gaze shifted from Marian to my husband and me. "Anarchy, dear." Dear? "Did you threaten Marian?"

"Nope." He popped the "p."

Marian turned. "You did! You said you'd have me arrested."

"Not a threat, Mrs. Dixon. A warning. You're trespassing, and you assaulted my wife."

Mother stiffened.

"She poked me," I explained.

For an instant, a glimmer of humor danced in Mother's eyes. But that couldn't be right.

"Marian, it seems wise to do as Anarchy asked."

"But my house! My house burned. There's a body. And it's Ellison's fault!"

The air around Mother froze. Frost coated the grass at her feet. Icicles hung from the branches of nearby trees. "Pardon me?"

"Your daughter attracts trouble." Marian's voice got louder with each word. "She attracts bodies."

Ice encased Mother's beautifully manicured nails then reached for her eyes. "Ellison is not responsible for the fire. Her husband saved your fool cat. If you dare repeat that allegation again, I will file a libel suit on her behalf, and a burned house will be the least of your problems."

Marian said nothing. I wondered if her vocal chords were as frozen as my yard.

"Are we clear?" Mother arched an imperious brow.

Marian gave a tiny nod.

"Excellent." Mother turned her attention to me. "A robe, Ellison? At this time of morning." She shook her head as if I were a hopeless case. "Do you at least have coffee made?"

"Of course." I waved her toward the front door. "Please, come in."

Mother breezed through the front door.

Marian stumbled across the street, headed for the Carsons'.

A moment later, Mother, who wore a pale yellow summer suit and white silk blouse with a floppy bowtie, sat on my living room couch and sipped her coffee. "Those muffins look delicious. Which do you recommend?"

"Lemon poppyseed." Did she intend to ignore the scene on my front lawn?

She made her selection and put the muffin on a Spode dessert plate. "It's quite clear your neighbor has lost her mind." She glanced at Anarchy, who lingered in the doorway. "I commend you for defending Ellison." Her shoulders straightened. Who knew they could get any straighter? "No one pokes my daughter. No one libels my daughter. The nerve of that woman."

"She found out her house burned down, then her husband left her. All in the space of five minutes."

"That's no excuse, Ellison." Mother took a small sip of coffee. "Where's Grace?"

"Asleep."

"And Max?"

"Also asleep."

Her brows rose.

"I'll check on him." Anarchy made a hasty retreat.

That left Mother and me alone with an elephant. I searched for something to say. "I bought a new desk."

"Oh?"

"Would you like to see it?" I stood. "It's in the study."

She followed me across the hall and stopped in her tracks when she saw Aaron's work. "Ellison..."

"I know."

"Where did you find it?"

"Handmade."

Mother's fingers stroked the desk's surface. "Where?"

"The artist's name is Aaron Minton."

"Just desks?"

"Bedroom sets, tables, chests, chairs."

"Local?"

"In Raytown."

She shrugged. "Nobody's perfect."

"I'll take you sometime."

"This week."

I had a feeling Aaron would soon have more customers than he could handle. "I'm glad you stopped by." I had no idea what prompted Mother's visit, but I was deeply grateful she'd arrived when she did. Arresting Marian after her dual misfortunes would have been awful. "Thank you for coming to my rescue."

"Always, dear."

Brnng, brnng.

I picked up the phone that sat on Henry's old desk. "Hello."

"Ellison, it's Virginia Minton. I'm calling to thank you for last night. We had a lovely evening."

"We did, too. We'll have to do it again soon."

"Yes, please. Next time at our place. Quick question."

"Yes?"

"The boy and the dog. What was his name?"

"Beau and Finn." I'd expected her to request Aggie's shortcake recipe. Aaron had devoured two servings.

"Which is which?"

"Beau is the boy. Finn is the dog."

"The boy. He looked so familiar."

"Beau is Whit Riley's son."

Virginia was quiet for long seconds. "No wonder he looked familiar." Her voice sounded odd.

But before I could ask if something was wrong, Mother

cleared her throat. "Virginia, my mother stopped by for a visit. May I call you back?"

"No need. I just wanted to thank you."

"Our pleasure. Also, I showed Mother the desk, and she'd like to speak to Aaron about a few projects."

"Thank you. For everything."

We both hung up, and I turned and faced Mother. "That was Virginia Minton." I did not add *née Wycliff*. "Her husband made the desk."

"You had dinner with them?"

"They stayed after they delivered the desk."

She nodded. Being kind to tradespeople was expected. Dinner was a bit much, but Aaron Minton was an artist, so she'd let it pass.

"It was nice of you to stop by."

There it was again—that unexpected glimmer of humor in Mothers eyes. "That reminds me of the reason I'm here. Your father can't play golf today. His back is bothering him."

For once, I was grateful she hadn't just called.

When I came downstairs after taking a shower, Anarchy and Beau were in the back yard with Max and Finn.

I joined them and watched as the dogs tugged on a strip of fabric. "What do they have?"

"A tie," said Beau.

Max jerked his head, and Finn's teeth lost their grip on the ruined tie. My dog ran to me and dropped his prize at my feet.

I stared at the mangled silk, a crimson, that was really more maroon, with white diagonal stripes. "Beau, where did Finn get this tie?"

"I'm not sure." Beau shrugged. "I guess in our back yard."

Anarchy's gaze met mine. "Why do you ask?"

I recognized the tie's pattern. "It's a Harvard tie."

"And?"

"Grant Wyclif attended Harvard." Whit attended Northwestern.

"Hey, Beau. Any idea how long Finn has had this?" Anarchy asked.

"A while," Beau replied. "At least a week."

I took a step toward the kitchen door. "I'll call Kate."

Anarchy nodded, and I hurried to my desk, found her number, and dialed.

"Thomas residence."

"Kate, it's Ellison. When you saw Grant, what was he wearing?"

"A suit." Her answer was immediate. "Navy, I think."

"Did he wear a tie?"

"I'm sure he did."

"Do you remember what it looked like?"

She paused. "Striped? Sorry, but I can't remember the colors."

"You've been incredibly helpful. Thank you."

"Everything okay?"

"Fine."

"Because those are oddly specific questions. Have you seen Grant?"

"Not recently. I'll tell you more when I can."

"I hold you to that."

We hung up, and I returned to the back yard where Anarchy had taken possession of what remained of the tie.

"Grant wore a suit and a striped tie."

"Who's Grant?" Beau sat on the ground between Max and Finn. The dogs looked winded and happy.

"An old friend," I told him.

"The tie belongs to him?"

"Maybe."

"I wondered how it got there. Dad said it wasn't his."

"Your dad saw the tie?"

His cheeks colored. "I showed it to him. If Finn stole it…" He scratched behind his dog's ears. "If Finn stole it, it's better to fess up than have Dad discover it."

"Did your dad say anything about the tie?"

"He told me to bring Finn over here."

Had Grant gone to see Whit? If so, why had he parked at the bottom of the street? If not Whit, then… "Oh."

"A light bulb just turned on above your head, Mrs. Jones. Stop it, Finn." Beau pushed on the dog who relentlessly nudged him for more scratches.

Anarchy had a light bulb of his own. "Ellison, may I speak with you inside?"

Beau bit his lower lip. "Am I in trouble?"

"Not in the least," I promised. "We're going to talk for a minute, then I'll fix you an extra-large helping of strawberry shortcake."

"With whipped cream?"

"Absolutely."

We stepped into the kitchen, and I grabbed the edge of the counter. "Tippy and Grant?"

"It appears so."

Why was I surprised? "For how long?" I glanced out the window at the back yard. "That poor kid. His parents were already awful. And now it looks as if Whit is a killer."

Anarchy's shoulders sagged.

My fingers tightened on the counter. "So, what happened? Whit confronted Grant about the affair, killed him, and burned his body? That explains why Tippy has been off these past few weeks."

His nod was grim.

"What now?" I asked.

"I call for back-up, then go over to the Rileys' house. Can you keep Beau here?"

"Absolutely." My heart ached for Beau. His father would go to prison. His mother was a mess. "There are lots of victims in a murder."

"True." He brushed a kiss across my forehead then picked up the phone.

I listened to his request for back-up. When he hung up, I lifted my brows. "Well?"

"There's a patrol car two minutes away. I'll meet them out front."

"Be careful."

"Always."

He left, and I turned to the fridge, taking out a large bowl of cut strawberries and a small bowl of whipped cream. I centered an enormous piece of Aggie's shortcake on a plate, covered the cake with strawberries, and glanced out the window.

Finn and Max tugged on the same rope they'd had last night.

A shiver started at my nape then descended my spine. I left Beau's treat on the counter, hurried to Anarchy's office, and found Virginia's phone number.

She picked up on the first ring. "Minton's Fine Furniture. How may I help you?"

"Virginia, it's Ellison."

"Ellison." She sounded surprised.

"I have a question."

"Go ahead."

"Did Beau really remind you of Whit?"

Her silence was an answer.

"He reminded you of Grant."

"Yes, but it was the dog. I was being fanciful."

"Tippy and Grant were having an affair."

"For ten years?" She groaned. "Fine. That boy looks so much

like Grant at that age that when I first saw him, I thought it was Grant."

What a mess. "Listen, Beau is in the back yard and I promised him strawberry shortcake. I need to go. I'll call you when I know more."

In the kitchen, I practically drowned Beau's strawberry shortcake in whipped cream.

I stared at the plate and resisted burying my head in my arms. That poor, sweet boy. Extra whipped cream didn't matter, not when his world was about to be turned upside down.

You and Anarchy can be here for him. Grace, too.

"But—"

He'll need stability and a place where he feels safe. You can fill that need.

"How did you get so smart?"

I run on coffee.

With a grateful nod to my countertop mage, I carried the plate out to the patio.

Beau met me at the wrought-iron table, and his eyes rounded. "Wow."

"You said you liked whipped dream."

He nodded with almost-ten-years-old vigor. "I do."

"Then, enjoy."

"Beau?" It was Tippy's voice, and it was coming from the gate to the front yard.

"We're in back," I called. Then I said to Beau, "Go ahead and eat. I'll keep your mother busy."

Beau dug in.

Tippy wandered into the back yard. She wore shorts and a tee-shirt and a pair of flip-flops, and her eyes were slightly crazy.

The dogs lolled at Beau's feet in hopes he'd drop dollops of whipped cream on the bricks.

And I swallowed a sigh that rose from my toes. "Tippy."

"Ellison." She glanced at her son, then pressed her hand to her throat. "Can we talk?"

I forced a smile for Beau's benefit. "Absolutely. Would you care for something to drink? Tab? Iced tea? Lemonade?"

"An Arnold Palmer?"

"Of course. Why don't you join me in the kitchen? You can fix your own."

We left Beau, and I led the woman, who quite possibly had killed his biological father, into my home.

CHAPTER SIXTEEN

I leaned against the counter and watched as Tippy adjusted the ratio of iced tea and lemonade in her Arnold Palmer.

"So." She swirled the two liquids together, and the ice clinked in her glass.

I crossed my arms. "So."

"Your husband is at my house. How did he figure it out?"

"Finn brought us a Harvard tie."

"That dog has caused more trouble than should be possible."

"I empathize."

"But Max is smart. Finn is as dumb as a box of rocks."

We had bigger issues than her dog's lack of intelligence. "You and Grant?"

She sighed. "It started in college. We were two midwestern kids on the east coast, and we gravitated toward each other."

"And Whit?"

"He was so far away. Neither of us wanted to hurt him." She studied the floor as if the secrets of the universe were written on its surface. "I loved them both."

"After college? Did the affair continue?"

"No."

I pursed my lips.

"We saw each other at a reunion weekend. Whit didn't come. Olivia was sick. Grant and I reconnected. Whit and I had gotten to the point where I felt invisible. Grant saw me."

"And after that?"

"We've been together, off and on, ever since."

"Beau?"

She paled. "I don't know."

"But you suspect."

She nodded.

"Does Whit suspect?"

"No. At least he didn't until recently."

"Why did Grant come to Kansas City?"

"He wanted me to leave Whit."

"And?"

"I told him 'no.' He didn't take it well."

"Grant came to see you the Tuesday before the fire." The afternoon that Kate saw him.

"It's why I was late picking up Beau. By the time I got rid of Grant and got to the pool, Jane had already given Beau a ride home."

"And the meet? I saw Whit but not you."

"I told Whit I didn't feel well. Grant came over so we could talk."

"He took off his tie?"

The way she flushed said he'd taken off much more than his tie. "Finn has a thing for ties. I didn't realize he'd swiped it."

"What happened, Tippy?"

"He threatened to tell Whit. Ten years of betrayal. I couldn't do that to him."

Except she had done exactly that. She'd betrayed her husband for a decade. She'd gotten pregnant with Grant's baby and allowed Whit to believe Beau was his.

"Don't you dare judge me. You and Henry had a terrible marriage."

"So I know how it feels to be betrayed."

Bright spots burned on her cheeks. "Did Henry belittle you? Make you feel small? Worthless?"

On a daily basis. "Did you kill Grant?"

She avoided my gaze.

Oh dear Lord. I hated being right. "What happened?"

"Whit killed him." There were some (most notably Mother) who called me gullible. Maybe they were right. But I wasn't falling for that lie.

"You've already betrayed him. Are you really going to frame him for murder?"

"Beau. If I go to jail, what happens to Beau? You've seen how Whit treats him."

She should have thought about that before she killed Grant. "Grant's sister lives in Kansas City."

"What? Virginia?"

"Yes."

She sank onto the nearest stool and rested her elbows on the counter. Then she dropped her head into her hands. "We fought. He grabbed me, and I pushed him. He stumbled and hit his head. Then he didn't move."

"You didn't call an ambulance?"

"I was trying to save my marriage."

"To the man who belittles you?"

"Without Whit, what do I have? No job. No money. I've been unfaithful. No court would give me a decent divorce settlement." She looked up, and her eyes beseeched me. To understand. To forgive. To pretend this conversation never happened.

"What did you do?"

"I knew Marian and Leonard were gone because she asked me to take care of her cat. I dragged his body to their house."

"You had a key."

"Yes. When everyone was asleep, I went back and set the fire. Macrame is surprisingly flammable."

I simply stared at her. Rather than own up to her sins, she'd let Grant die, burned down the Dixons' house, and destroyed her son's childhood. And I could not detect an ounce of remorse.

"What now?" she asked.

"Why don't you go spend some time with your son?" Beau deserved a few more minutes before his world imploded. "I'll call Anarchy."

Tippy stepped outside, and I poured myself a cup of coffee.

I don't believe her. Righteous indignation deepened Mr. Coffee's voice.

"You don't believe she killed Grant?"

Oh, she killed him. But the way she describes what happened makes it sound like self-defense. That's the part I doubt.

"Me, too."

Are you going to call Anarchy?

I glanced out the window to the patio where Tippy sat with her son. "Yes. Drat."

What?

"I don't know the Rileys' phone number." I hurried to my desk in the family room, grabbed the club directory, and dialed their number.

"Hello." A stranger's voice answered the phone. A man's voice. One of the police officers?

"This is Ellison Jones. I need to speak with my husband. It's an emergency."

"He's busy, Mrs. Jones."

"It's an emergency."

"He's interviewing a murder suspect."

"Yes, I know. But the actual killer is at our house."

He scoffed.

I channeled Mother. "I want to speak with my husband.

Anarchy will be displeased when he hears you refused to tell him I called."

"Then I guess he'll be displeased." He hung up.

I ground my teeth. Where had I gone wrong? That always worked for Mother. I went to the windows and searched for Tippy and Beau. They were still sitting at the table. Beau had finished his strawberry shortcake, and his fingers were laced across his belly.

If I cut through the Dixons' yard, I could be at the Rileys' house in under two minutes. I hurried back to the kitchen, through the front hallway, and outside. Then I ran.

My finger jabbed the Rileys' doorbell so hard that the first knuckle bent backward.

A ridiculously tall, uniformed police officer answered the door.

"I need to speak with Detective Jones. I'm his wife."

He looked down at me. "I already told you. He's busy."

"Anarchy!" I yelled loud enough to disturb the birds in the trees. "Anarchy!"

"Be quiet!"

"What part of emergency don't you understand?"

Anarchy appeared next to the idiot officer.

"Ellison, what's wrong?"

"Whit didn't do it."

"Then who?" His face sagged as the realization hit him. "Where is she?"

"Our house. I tried phoning you, but he—" I pointed at the officer who'd refused to connect us "—wouldn't put the call through."

"Where's Beau?"

"In the back yard with the dogs." My stomach sank. "You don't think she'd hurt him?" I took off running. Through the Rileys' backyard. Through the gate that connected their property to the Dixons'. Past the charred remains of the Dixons' house.

Anarchy ran with me.

I skipped the front door and raced through the gate to the back yard.

Beau held a dessert plate on his lap while two happy dogs licked off the remaining whipped cream.

Tippy was gone.

"Beau." I gasped for breath. "Where's your mom?"

"She said she had to go."

"Did she say where?" asked Anarchy.

"No. She told me she loved me, then she left." He studied our expressions.

I saw the moment when resignation settled onto his young shoulders. They bent. "She's not coming back, is she?" His voice was small.

I pulled him into a hug and rubbed circles on his back as he sobbed.

"I feel like an idiot. I shouldn't have left her alone."

Anarchy, who sat next to me on the couch in our family room, took my hand in his. "It's not your fault, Ellison. We'll find her."

I'd told him everything Tippy told me. "What happens now?"

"We find her and arrest her for murdering Grant."

"She'll claim self-defense."

"Dragging his body to a neighbor's house then burning that house down makes that claim harder to believe. Especially when she left the body there for hours before she started the fire."

"She said she loved them all. Whit and Grant and Beau,

but...but she only cared about herself. She had to keep her secret to protect herself from the fall-out."

Anarchy pulled me closer to him. "I wish you'd stop confronting killers. What if she'd decided to kill you, too?"

"Maybe it really was an accident. Maybe she pushed Grant, not knowing he'd hit his head. When he died, she panicked." I liked that version.

"Maybe she whacked him with a fireplace poker."

"My version is better."

"Look at the bright side," said Anarchy.

"There's a bright side?"

"The Clarkes are no longer suspects."

Max, who sprawled on the carpet near our feet, lifted his head and stared at us.

"What about Beau?"

Anarchy's grip on my shoulder tightened. "What about him?"

"I hate to think of him with Whit. He's Grant's son, and Virginia knows—"

Ding, dong.

We glanced at each other.

"Expecting anyone?" he asked.

"No. You?"

"Nope."

We rose from the couch and walked to the front hall together..

Whit Riley stood on our front stoop. The man looked awful. His cheeks were haggard. His eyes had sunk into his skull. And beneath his tan, his skin looked sallow. He was so broken I didn't see how he'd ever put himself back together.

"Whit." I didn't know what else to say.

"I'm leaving. I need to get away from here. My parents have a cabin in Wisconsin. I'm going to stay there."

I, I, I. No one thought for his son's pain. He only cared about himself. "What about Beau?"

Whit stared at me with dead eyes. "I need to be alone."

Another *I*. "His mother left him. Now, you too?" Anger on Beau's behalf sizzled in my veins.

"I can't." He shook his head. "I can't. Will you take him? Just until I get my head straight?"

"Yes." Anarchy's response was immediate. "We'll keep him."

"And Finn?"

"The dog, too," I replied.

"I'll help him pack then bring them over."

He turned away, and Anarchy closed the door.

The enormity of what we'd just agreed to hit me. "What do we do?"

"We give that boy all our love and support." He pulled me to his chest. "He's going to need it."

My heart swelled. "You're the best man I know."

He kissed the tip of my nose. "And you're the best woman I know."

"If Whit doesn't come back?"

"Then we talk to Virginia."

"About?"

"Awarding us custody."

That was a huge, life-changing decision, but it felt simple. Right. My arms circled Anarchy's waist, and I snuggled closer. "Mother will have a fit."

With my check pressed against Anarchy's chest, I couldn't see his smile, but I knew it was there. "That's just a bonus."

Fields' Guide to Pharaohs

Fields' Guide to Dirty Money

Fields' Guide to Smuggling

Fields' Guide to Secrets

www.ingramcontent.com/pod-product-compliance
Lightning Source LLC
Chambersburg PA
CBHW072132300726
48975CB00003B/1026